# Praise for Yvonne Ventresca's

A 2017 Independent Publisher Book Award Gold Medal Winner
An October 2016 ALAN Pick

"Prepare your fingernails, because tension mounts quickly as Ella's reality is chipped away piece by piece by the strange series of events that are tied to her father. Is there a ghost, is she losing her mind, or is someone manipulating her? This one will keep you guessing."
—*Justine* Magazine

"Ventresca has carefully plotted a variety of twists and turns in this engrossing mystery that doesn't let up until the final pages. It's tense, scary, and, at times, upsetting, everything a supernatural thriller ought to be."
—Jeffrey Harr, ALAN

"While the clues are all there, readers will be guessing up to the very end of this riveting page-turner, as it shifts from the possibilities of supernatural connections to the all too possible implications of mental illness. Young adult readers will love this story, and librarians serving teens should have it in their collection."
—*VOYA*

"I raced through *Black Flowers, White Lies* in a single sitting. What a twisty thrill-ride!"
—April Henry, *New York Times*-bestselling author of *Girl, Stolen*

"With a compelling cast of characters and a mystery that'll have you turning pages, *Black Flowers, White Lies* is a book you don't want to miss!"
—Tiffany Schmidt, author of the Once Upon a Crime Family series

"*Black Flowers, White Lies* is not your typical YA thriller. It's beautifully written and tightly plotted, telling a story that manages to keep a tight, intimate hold on the reader by digging into some universal fears that aren't often explored in novels. An unnerving reminder that darkness—and even evil—often hides in plain sight."
—Jessica Warman, author of *Between*

"A captivating story of a girl facing unexplained events that shake her to her core, open up old wounds, and make her wonder what's real. Is it madness or haunting? You'll be turning pages until the end to find out. Highly recommended!"
—Maria E. Andreu, award-winning author of
*The Secret Side of Empty*

"A chilling tale of faith and deception. The supernatural scares kept me hooked, and the ending absolutely blew me away!"
—Joshua David Bellin, author of *Survival Colony 9*
and *Scavenger of Souls*

"*Black Flowers, White Lies* lures you in with charming characters and situations that seem innocuous until they become sinister. A great read from cover to cover."
—Dr. George Simon, bestselling author of *In Sheep's Clothing: Understanding and Dealing with Manipulative People*

"From Oscar the cat and the cute guy Blake to the little bit of romance, *Black Flowers, White Lies* was hard to put down. Filled with suspense, surprises, and even shock, this page turner will be a favorite for anyone who likes mystery, excitement, and cats."
—Jessica Nelson, *VOYA* Teen Reviewer

"There's twists and turns throughout this novel that [give] it a Hitchcock appeal."
— *YA Books Central*

"Ventresca does an excellent job of capturing an independent bookstore and Hoboken . . . A book with a smart ending."
—*Star Ledger*

"This psychological suspense . . . literally deserves time up on the 'big screen.'"
—Feathered Quill Book Reviews

"Completely satisfying. *Black Flowers, White Lies* compellingly and convincingly questions the links between mental illness and reality, revealing how fragile our understanding of and grip upon reality actually is."
—J.L. Powers, The Pirate Tree

"Readers will find the constant twists, intrigue and red herrings all blend to make for a dandy psychological thriller . . . This is a nice choice for both school and public library collections."
—*CMLD Kids/Teens Book Reviews*

"I loved this book. It's an incredibly fast read and I was so curious about what was going on and who was responsible (and there are, like, a ton of credible suspects). This book was an absolute delight."
—*KellyVision*

# Also by Yvonne Ventresca

## Pandemic

# BLACK FLOWERS, WHITE LIES

## YVONNE VENTRESCA

Sky Pony Press
New York

Sky Pony Press books may be purchased in bulk at special discounts for sales promotion, corporate gifts, fund-raising, or educational purposes. Special editions can also be created to specifications. For details, contact the Special Sales Department, Sky Pony Press, 307 West 36th Street, 11th Floor, New York, NY 10018 or info@ skyhorsepublishing.com.

Sky Pony® is a registered trademark of Skyhorse Publishing, Inc.®, a Delaware corporation.

Visit our website at www.skyponypress.com.

10 9 8 7 6 5 4 3 2 1

The Library of Congress has catalogued the hardcover edition as follows:

Names: Ventresca, Yvonne, author.
Title: Black flowers, white lies / Yvonne Ventresca.
Description: New York : Skyhorse Publishing, Inc., [2016] | Summary: Ella Benton's psychic connection with her long-dead father may mean that a series of mysterious, increasingly sinister events are a warning from him, or a sign that she is following him into madness.
Identifiers: LCCN 2016023041 (print) | LCCN 2016051882 (ebook) | ISBN 9781510709881 (hc : alk. paper) | ISBN 9781510709973
Subjects: | CYAC: Supernatural--Fiction. | Fathers and daughters--Fiction. | Stepbrothers--Fiction. | Psychopaths--Fiction. | Remarriage--Fiction.
Classification: LCC PZ7.V564 Bl 2016 (print) | LCC PZ7.V564 (ebook) | DDC [Fic]--dc23

Cover design by Sarah Brody
Cover image credit iStock

Paperback ISBN: 978-1-5107-2596-6
Ebook ISBN: 978-1-5107-0997-3

Printed in the United States of America

Interior design by Joshua Barnaby

To Lauren and David,
With love

"There are two ways to be fooled. One is to believe what isn't true; the other is to refuse to believe what is true."

—Søren Kierkegaard

# 1

# BEAUTIFUL BOY

I approach Dad's tombstone with trepidation, then breathe a sigh of relief. No mysterious flowers wilt at his grave as I had feared. Last August, someone left fresh orange lilies for him throughout the month. I never figured out who. Then, in September, the flowers stopped appearing as suddenly as they started. I always wondered, with an odd mixture of anxiety and hope, if I would run into the other mourner— someone else who honored my father. But I never did.

Usually, the ritual of navigating the same cemetery rows, visiting Thomas Darren Benton, and putting a small rock on his headstone calms me. Now, the heat is relentless and sweat trickles down my back as I search for the perfect pebble. It needs to be a nice, roundish one. Despite the lilies left last summer, Dad wasn't a bouquet kind of guy.

I know this even though I never met him. He died before I was born, so I have no memories of him, only stories from Mom that I've heard so many times it feels like I was actually there. I see him beam during his graduation from veterinary school and feel his hand pat Mom's pregnant belly. I hear him pick my name from the baby book: Ariella, meaning lion, although Mom insists they nickname me Ella. I smell the damp on his clothes from the night he rescued Oscar the kitten from a storm drain and brought him home to stay. These recollections have been cobbled together into my own version of Dad for the last fifteen years.

Today the sky is gray and foreboding, but the occasional burst of wind does nothing to cool me. I finally find just the right rock nestled in a patch of grass and rub off the dirt with my fingers. My friend Jana taught me the tradition of leaving a stone as a way to mark my visits with something more permanent, more enduring than flowers.

I'm the only person who comes to his grave somewhat regularly, other than last summer's unknown mourner. I don't think Mom's been here since her engagement to Stanley, a non-reading, self-absorbed, stubby man. With the wedding only days away, Stanley's settled into our apartment, but each awkward conversation we have leaves me yearning for the father who painted my room a cheerful yellow, who created a mini-library of animal books to read to his future daughter.

I hesitate before BELOVED HUSBAND AND FATHER, rolling the pebble between my fingers, then place it in line with the last one, making it the eighth in a row. I let my hand linger against the cool granite. Next week is Dad's birthday, August 8. That number has been lucky for me since I was eight years old, when I could have died, but because of Dad's warning, I didn't.

The air gusts, whipping strands of hair across my face and scattering the pebbles to the ground. My skin prickles at the eerie timing before I realize that the wind has been stormy on and off throughout the day. Still, it spooks me because nothing has disturbed my markers in months. Until now. It's almost like Dad is giving me another sign.

The cemetery turns out to be more peaceful than home. I'm lounging across my bed checking my phone with Oscar purring beside me when—*bang*—Mom pounds on the adjacent wall. Oscar scampers to the top of my bookcase, his favorite spot in times of trouble.

The room next to mine serves as Mom's office, and since my soon-to-be-stepbrother is expected to arrive later tonight, she's fixing it up. Loudly.

I give up on coaxing Oscar down and move to the doorway. "What are you doing?"

"Look." She points with the hammer at two new pictures of the Manhattan skyline where a framed print of *The Cat in the Hat* used to be. Besides changing the wall decorations, she also cleared out the closet and moved her many piles of papers from the desk. "Do you think Blake will like it?"

I have no idea what Blake will like. The only photo I've even seen of him is one that Stanley keeps on his nightstand.

It's a faded picture of a young blond boy at the beach, smiling up at him.

"The room looks nice," I say. "But it's not like he's living here forever." Blake would only be staying with us for a few weeks until he moved into his dorm at NYU.

"I know. But I want this to feel like home for him."

She certainly cares a lot about this guy we've never met. The filing cabinet, the now-spotless desk, and the fax machine are the sole remnants of her office.

"After we find your dress today, I need to buy some blue sheets and maybe some towels, too," she says. "Are you ready to go?"

"Sure." I sigh quietly.

Our apartment building is directly across from the Hoboken PATH station. After a short train ride to the Newport Mall, I remember for the hundredth time why I hate shopping with Mom. Every dress she pulls off the rack is revolting. But the wedding is only days away. We need to find something suitable that won't forever embarrass me when I see the photos in years to come.

"How about this?" Mom holds up a mauve paisley thing with puffy sleeves, her eyes shiny with hope. "This color will look so flattering on you."

"Maybe." I don't want to hurt her feelings, so I purposely drift away to shop on my own. And then I see it: a pale yellow dress, strapless, with a flouncy skirt and sequins around the middle. The dress sparkles when I hold it against me. I can't wait to try it on.

Mom will hate it. She'll want me to look conservative for the small group of friends and family at her wedding. My strategy is to show her other dresses she'll hate even more. I find a black mini she'll say isn't long enough and a floral sundress she'll think is too casual.

When I get to the dressing room, Mom and three hideous pink dresses await.

I try on the minidress first, which she predictably declares too short. Luckily, the mauve one bunches at my waist. She likes the sundress, but not for the wedding.

I put on a blush-colored one.

"It's not bad," she says. "What do you think?"

"Too much lace. It's like wearing a tablecloth."

She nods in agreement.

Finally, I try on the yellow one and giggle with delight. I come out, posture perfect, feeling like a princess. "Isn't it beautiful?"

Mom frowns. "Strapless? You'd need something over it."

I twirl. "I have that silver sweater at home."

"Let's see the rose-colored one."

"Fiiine."

In the dressing room, I breathe deeply as I put on the last dress.

Her face lights up when I step out. "Ella! It's so pretty!

It brings a glow to your cheeks. And it's perfect with your coloring."

She calls it *my* coloring because I inherited Dad's brown hair and brown eyes instead of her fairness.

"The rose is all right," I say. "But don't you think the ruffles look too childish for a sophomore?"

"Honey. It's perfect for an *almost*-sophomore. And it's appropriate. The yellow one might be nice for a dance, but for the wedding . . ."

I close the curtain and put on my shorts and favorite T-shirt, the one with the tabby cat that says RESCUED IS MY FAVORITE BREED. It's her wedding, I remind myself. She should get to choose. I should be mature.

I walk out and hand her the ruffled dress.

"Thank you. It means a lot to me," Mom says. "I'll pay for this and go to the bedding department. Want to meet at the food court in an hour?"

"Sure."

I shake off my annoyance and detour into the accessories section, where my friend Grace had seen a cute wallet with kittens on it that she thought I'd like. I'm sifting through the clearance items when this guy approaches me, holding a bunch of ties. Whoa. He's tall and blond, and his white polo shirt shows off his tan.

"Excuse me," Beautiful Boy says. "I'm trying to decide between these?" His voice lilts into a question. His smile is friendly, his eyes deep brown and intense. "I suck at this kind of thing." He somehow manages to look model-perfect and sheepish at the same time. "Would you mind helping me pick one?"

I blink for a minute, staring at his face instead of the ties. My delayed response verges on awkward. "Okay," I say. "What are you wearing it with?"

"A gray suit."

I'm conscious of his eyes on me as I study the ones he's chosen. It makes it hard to think. None of the ties have any yellow, my favorite color. Maybe it's the dress shopping with Mom, but I point to the gray one with rose-colored diamond shapes. "I like this."

"Thanks."

I wish I could prolong our interaction somehow so that I can learn more about him. He lingers a too-short moment, then gives me another smile before he turns away.

I can't help feeling like something momentous has transpired. I'm a believer in karma and fate and the mysterious workings of the universe. As I watch Beautiful Boy walk away, I hope that meeting him again is meant to be.

# THE NEW
# NORMAL

I arrive at the food court first and wait. Once Mom gets there, we each buy a salad: me because it's vegan, and her because she's dieting for the wedding. While we eat, she shows me the navy-striped sheets she bought as if they are vaguely interesting. It's like being subjected to an itchy sweater. Is this instant sibling rivalry?

"Are you going with Stanley to the airport tonight to pick up Blake?" I ask.

"His flight lands late, around two in the morning. He said he'll take a cab. I think he wants to show up on his own instead of relying on his father."

"Why is he even coming to the wedding? I thought he and Stanley weren't talking."

I haven't heard Stanley mention Blake since he'd tried to fly his son out here for a fancy dinner and he never appeared. I had felt bad for Stanley. He'd wanted it to be the "special first meeting of our future blended family," but Blake's empty seat at the table turned it into a dismal night.

"I think they've worked through a lot of emotional issues. Stanley seems convinced this time will be different. Blake was young when his parents got divorced. He felt abandoned, I think." She rummages through a shopping bag, no doubt to change the subject. "Anyway, look what else I bought." She pulls out a blue plaid throw pillow.

"Great," I say, not bothering to fake much enthusiasm.

"What's going on with you today?" she asks. "You've been in a bad mood since you went out this morning. Where did you run off to, anyway?"

I'm a horrible liar, so I don't even try. "The cemetery."

She shakes her head, wordlessly conveying that I've disappointed her somehow by visiting Dad so recently. I tamp down the annoyance for the millionth time today. I have a right to visit the cemetery. Mom doesn't understand; my friends don't either. *He's been dead your whole life*, they say.

But especially in August, the month of his birth and death, the visits help me. It's an uncomplicated relationship, and being in the cemetery brings me peace, quiets the anxious thoughts that often scurry through my mind.

Mom and I don't speak on the walk to the PATH. By the door to the station, a homeless man sits on a piece of cardboard next to his German shepherd and a garbage bag of belongings. The dog looks well cared for but pants from the heat. I dig through Dad's worn leather messenger bag that I've been carrying lately and pull out some loose change.

"No," Mom says, steering me by the elbow.

"But the dog looks thirsty!"

"I know you want to help. You have a kind heart. But it's better to give money to a homeless organization instead."

I yank my arm free and keep walking. I desperately want to avoid an argument in the days before she goes away for her honeymoon. As much as Mom irritates me, she's all the family I've got. We've had lots of fun times through the years, I remind myself. Like our trip to Disney World and the time she drove me all the way to Alliance, Ohio, to visit the Feline Historical Museum.

I need to survive the next five days without a major blowup. Then: freedom. She'll be on her honeymoon, I'll stay with Grace, and when Mom returns, we'll reach some new type of equilibrium. I hope.

"Would you mind bringing the shopping bags up?" she asks when we reach our apartment building. "I'm due at the store by three. What are your plans for this afternoon? I could use some help there." Mom owns Benton Books a few blocks away. When I turned fifteen, she finally agreed to start paying me by the hour. But I checked the calendar on the kitchen bulletin board this morning and I'm off today.

"I'm going to Grace's."

"Can you skip it? Please? I'll feel better leaving for the

honeymoon if the store is in good shape. And you'll spend time with her while I'm away."

"I guess I can see Grace later." I sigh, but restrain myself from the eye roll.

"Thank you." She gives me a hug and some of the resentment fades away. This must be a nerve-racking time for her. I need to be understanding.

At home, I put Mom's bags on the counter. I hang up my new dress, hoping it will somehow look better than it did in the store.

No. It's still dreadful.

Stanley's at work. I plop on the couch, relishing this time alone. You wouldn't think going from two people to three in our home would be such a big deal, but it's been an adjustment. Oscar jumps up and rubs his head against me. He's a beautiful tabby, black and tan, with white around his nose and a belly the color of coffee. I pet him as I absorb the happy silence.

Would I feel this way if it were Dad living here instead of Stanley?

For a moment, I find myself lost in the world of what-might-have-been. If only Dad's emergency surgery hadn't run late. If only he had skipped the meeting afterward and come straight home. If only the drunk had given someone else his car keys and their paths hadn't tragically collided. My life would be different. *I* would be different, somehow an enhanced, better version of me.

Grace calls, interrupting my daydream.

"Hey," she says. "Are you home? How was the mall?"

"One ugly dress later . . ."

"Oh no. You were afraid of that."

Kids screech in the background. "How's your afternoon going?" I ask. Grace is working at a daycare for the summer.

"The paint will never come off my sneakers," she says. "One hour left. See you soon?"

"Sorry, Mom needs me at the bookstore. She's extra demanding today."

"Ugh. We have no social lives."

"That reminds me. I did have a brief encounter at the mall." I tell her all about Beautiful Boy. "Cross your fingers I somehow see him again. Hey, maybe we should have our Tarot cards read. I want to go to the place on Bloomfield."

"Because that will tell you all about future romance?" Grace teases.

I ignore her, and we hang up with a promise to talk later.

Grace has been my friend since our moms took us trick-or-treating together in second grade. She told the best ghost stories that afternoon, and I was hooked. Together, we explored all things paranormal. Somewhere along the way, though, she stopped believing. I never did.

After dinner, Mom, Stanley, and I play a family round of Boggle. Mom and I used to play backgammon, but since it's only a two-person game, we've shifted our routine to include Stanley. Apparently, he has a horrible vocabulary, including short words. I don't know how Mom can stand his pouting when he doesn't win.

"I could teach you to play chess, El," he suggests after losing again. "I taught Blake and we used to have such enjoyable matches." His voice is hopeful. "I can't believe he's on his way. It will be great to see him."

"Yes," I say. "Since it's been so many years."

"Ella!" Mom chides me like I've said something untrue.

"It's okay," Stanley says. "We haven't had the closest relationship since the divorce. It was a nasty breakup. I gave up on fighting Veronique to see him when work moved me away. I should have tried harder. And last year . . . well, now our relationship will be different."

Stanley draws a big X through his losing word list. "It's water under the proverbial bridge. Blake will be here for the wedding. It's a wonderful thing! And NYU is so close. After school starts, he can join us for Sunday dinners."

Mom raises her eyebrows, which means the weekly meal idea is new to her, too. *Fabulous*.

Later that night, I peek into Mom's office. She made the bed with the striped sheets and the plaid throw pillow, with the comforter folded back like in a hotel. The closet is opened, showing a neat line of empty plastic hangers.

I hope Blake isn't a jerk. If he expects to be treated like royalty, I'll die.

Resting in bed, I check my phone. Grace has sent me a photo of the dress she's wearing to the wedding. *Nice*, I respond, but she doesn't answer. I try to reach Jana, but she's spending August at her grandmother's, where cell phones are considered evil. A Month of Misery, she calls it. At least she knows what to expect. Unlike me, entering unknown family territory. This is my new normal, I guess. At least when I leave for college in three years, Mom won't be by herself. I've thought about how hard it would be to leave her alone, but now she'll have Stanley to keep her company. I drift asleep to the sound of Mom and Stanley talking about centerpieces and seating arrangements.

I sleep late the next morning, waking at eleven to pounding rain. Oscar pads into the kitchen ahead of me, eager for his breakfast. I'm still rubbing my eyes when his hiss jolts me awake. When I see the cause of his hissing, I stiffen.

Sitting in my seat, sipping from my favorite cat mug, is Beautiful Boy.

# 3

# THE READING

I stare at the guy I'd desperately hoped to meet again, who is somehow here in the kitchen talking to Mom and Stanley. I'm suddenly conscious of the fact that I haven't brushed my teeth or my hair and that I'm wearing shorts and a sleep shirt with Felix the Cat on it. At least I slipped on a strapless bra before emerging.

Stanley practically jumps from his seat to introduce us. "Good morning, Ella! Glad you finally joined the living."

Blake stands to shake my hand. "Nice to meet you," he says.

"Hi," I manage. If he's as surprised as I am, he doesn't show it. My cheeks flush as I remember my attraction to him. Embarrassed at the memory, I'm relieved he doesn't say anything about seeing him at the mall. Maybe he doesn't even remember talking to me yesterday.

"Does anyone want breakfast?" Stanley asks. "Blake, do you still like Lucky Charms?"

"Sure," he says, sitting down. "I'm not hungry yet, though."

"Right, right. Let me know when you want some." Stanley smiles at him like when he finally manages a rare Boggle win.

Mom pours me coffee with one sugar in her READING IS MY SUPERPOWER mug. She may have awful taste in dresses, but at least she has no objection to my occasional caffeine consumption.

"Thanks, Mom." I take grateful sips. Oscar weaves insistently between my legs, so I put the mug down long enough to feed him. Then I take the empty seat at the table, across from *my* seat, which is occupied by the boy-formerly-known-as-beautiful.

I study him and his father. Blake is lean muscle compared to Stanley's slight paunch. They do have the same strong chin and the same intense brown eyes. Compared to Stanley's enthusiasm, Blake's tone and body language seem reserved. It reminds me of the first time I got scratched at the animal shelter, how the next few times I used extra caution volunteering with the cats. Blake is wary but polite as he answers Stanley's questions about graduation, NYU registration, and his upcoming classes.

While Blake asks Mom about the wedding arrangements—her favorite topic—the coffee finally kicks my brain into gear. Wasn't his flight supposed to arrive late last night? How was he even at the mall yesterday?

"About thirty people in total," Mom says. "Stanley

explained it would be hard for you to invite friends with everybody heading off to college. Don't worry. Only one of Ella's friends can make it. Right, El?"

Mom gives me a pointed look that mandates I join the conversation. Blake smiles at me, the same smile from yesterday. I find it hard to meet his eyes.

"Yes, my friend Grace will be there," I say. "With her parents and sister."

*Grace. Oh no.* I had called her and raved about the guy at the mall, who is actually my soon-to-be family. Awkward, awkward, awkward. Of course, I didn't realize who he was then. But I can't let her know. She'll tease me forever.

"We want it to be an intimate affair," Stanley says.

The phrase "intimate affair" makes me blush. I fight the urge to giggle inappropriately. "Excuse me," I mumble, rushing to the bathroom. I splash cold water on my face and decide to stay here as long as possible.

Wow. Today is going to suck.

Grace agrees to have our Tarot cards read in the afternoon. Getting out of the house outweighs putting up with her skepticism. Today's cat shirt reads YOU HAVE TO BE KITTEN ME RIGHT MEOW, which feels appropriate. You have to be kidding me that Blake is Beautiful Boy. I manage to avoid him until I'm about to leave. He's leaning against the kitchen counter, texting and suppressing a yawn.

"You must be tired after the late flight," I say, soft enough so that Mom and Stanley can't hear.

He leans close enough for me to smell—the ocean? His cologne reminds me of jumping waves at the beach. "I had some things to take care of, so I took an earlier flight. You can keep a secret, right?" He gives me an earnest smile, as if my cooperation means the world to him.

"Cross my heart," I say, closing the door gently behind me. What is wrong with me? *Cross my heart?* I sound like I'm in kindergarten.

The rain has stopped, and I have a little time before I need to meet Grace. I stroll down Washington Street and, without really planning it, somehow find myself at the entrance to Hoboken Hill Cemetery. I decide to go in quickly, just for a minute.

As I approach Dad's grave, I see them: dark flowers in front of his headstone. I shiver, checking for who might have left them, but no one else is around.

The flowers are disturbing. Why black? I know black roses can symbolize death. But the floppy, outstretched petals don't resemble roses, and death is a bit redundant in a cemetery.

Pebbles are scattered nearby, probably the same ones I used before. I pick one and place it in the center of the headstone, but I don't linger. As I hurry to Grace's, I debate whether or not to mention the cemetery visit to her.

"Nice cat shirt," she says, locking the door behind her. She lives in a detached three-story brownstone, which is the closest thing to a house in Hoboken. "But isn't it from seventh grade?" She scrunches her mouth in a way that suggests I have questionable taste.

I tug at the bottom, stretching it down. "I love this shirt!" Even if I were tempted to tell her anything about the cemetery, the insult makes up my mind.

The Tarot card place is at least a fifteen-minute walk from her house. Grace talks steadily on the way. "Can you believe Piper went through my closet again? That blue cami I couldn't find? It was crumpled on her floor. How could she think she'd ever pull off wearing it in her training bra? Makes me wish for a brother." She pauses. "Hey! Did you meet your new brother today?"

*Ack.* "Yes. Blake was at breakfast. He seems nice."

"That's it?"

"It's weird to have an instant family member. We didn't really talk much." I point down the street to change the subject. "We're almost there."

The building is brick, nondescript, except for the fluorescent blue PSYCHIC sign glowing in the ground-level window.

"So, this place opened recently?" Grace asks.

I'm sure she thinks it's cheesy. "The store has been here but I learned about the Tarot reader online. He's new and supposed to be amazingly accurate." I've had my palm read by a gypsy-looking woman at a street fair, but never had a Tarot reading.

"What are you going to ask about? The beautiful boy and your next romance?"

I'm glad she can't see my face as she follows me inside. I'm sure it's blazing red.

I recognize the owner, a tall woman who always looks like she's stepped out of a sportswear catalog with her coordinated shorts and running tops. She stands behind the counter of the narrow, brightly lit shop.

"Why don't you go first? My treat," I say to Grace. I brought some of my bookstore earnings for this.

We ask for two Tarot readings and Grace follows the woman through a curtained doorway into the back room. The owner returns, resuming her place behind the register.

I browse to pass the time. Books like *Healing with Gems*, *Feng Shui*, and *Exploring Inner Self with Tarot* line the shelves. A round table covered in lace displays aromatherapy oils. One of the floral scents reminds me of Mom. I sniff each of them until the smells blur and my head aches.

A new jewelry display catches my eye—a sparkly glass bowl filled with rings. They're all so pretty, it's hard to decide which I'd choose. I reach in and pull one out without looking. It's a black flower carved in stone. *Obsidian*, the label says. *Helps contact with the spirit world.*

Goose bumps cover my arms. Another black flower. Did I want more contact with the spirit world? I secretly hope that Dad watches out for me, kind of like a guardian angel. When Grace emerges from the back, I quickly bury the ring under the others in the bowl.

"Your turn." She says it with a tiny smirk, as if our whole adventure is silly.

My hands tremble with anticipation as I enter the dim room. A man with cloudy blue eyes waits at a dark wooden table. A white cane rests against the side of his chair. The online article praised his accurate readings, but no one mentioned that he's blind.

"Hi," I say quietly.

He motions to a chair opposite him. "Please sit."

The corners of the Tarot cards are marked with braille. He sorts the cards into random piles. "I'm cleansing them to remove leftover energy. Is there anything you want me to focus on in your reading?"

There are so many things I want to know. Will I have a boyfriend during sophomore year? Will I eventually get accepted into vet school? I think of the obsidian ring. Is it really possible to contact spirits? But none of those questions feel right when I try to verbalize them. "My family," I finally say.

He nods, passing the stack of cards to me. "Touch as many cards as you can, concentrating on thoughts of the family member you want to know about."

*Dad.* As I gently shuffle the cards, I think about the mini-album of photos I made when I was eight. I stole the snapshots of him from a scrapbook Mom keeps on the top shelf of her closet. I envision my favorite picture of Dad standing outside at the pier, looking toward the Hudson River. He's smiling away from the camera as if he knows a wonderful secret. I like to imagine he was daydreaming about me, his future daughter, when Mom caught his shy smile.

But his life was cut short, and soon Mom will be remarried. Stanley and Blake intrude on my thoughts, and it's hard to focus. I hand back the cards. He deals them out, touching the braille on each one. The silence lasts long enough to make me shift in my seat.

"Interesting," he finally says. He taps a card that displays matching towers with a passageway between them. Two menacing dogs block the path. "This shows danger."

I jiggle my foot nervously beneath the table. Tiny flowers line the base of the towers. They might be black, but they're too small and the room's too dark to tell for sure.

"You have a brief doorway of opportunity. You can create safety," he says. "But it will be difficult. Beware of betrayal. The cards indicate that you'll need to rely on your strength."

On the card labeled "Strength," a woman in a pale, flowing dress holds a lion's head with her hands as if to close its mouth. Am I the woman? Or the lion, like my name—Ariella? I don't have the courage to ask.

"Thank you." I stand, ready to leave.

"One last thing. I'm sensing . . . it feels like above." He gestures his hand in a circle over his head. "Whatever trials you face, you may get help from above."

*Above*. Just like I imagined—my dad in a mystical, heavenly world, somehow looking out for me. I don't want my longing to taint the reading, though, to make connections that aren't there. Dad had helped me avoid danger once before. I hope I don't need his help again.

# 4

# BROKEN

Grace and I linger outside her building. She makes fun of everything the blind man said: danger, betrayal, strength. It is lost on her, the fact that the Tarot reader doesn't have regular sight, but could have a different type of vision.

"I wonder what he meant by above." I don't mention that it might refer to Dad. Grace is too skeptical already and that would give her another reason to scoff at me.

"Maybe something religious?" she says. "Anyway, the psychic could be wrong. You know, Houdini—"

"Yeah, I know, I know. He exposed fake psychics." We've had this discussion before. I fold my arms across my chest. "What about your reading?" I ask. "What do you think the envy refers to, and the strong bonds weakening?"

She doesn't answer.

"What?" Now I've made her angry.

"If I believed in this type of thing," she says with a touch of condescension, "I'd think he was talking about my dress for the wedding. You hate the dress your mom picked for you. But what about mine?"

"What about it?"

"I texted you the picture and your answer was a single word."

I squeeze her arm. "Grace, I'm fine with your dress."

"You're sure? I thought you'd be jealous."

Does she want me to be jealous? Is that why she keeps going on about it? "I'm happy you'll look beautiful."

"Thanks. And I'll get to meet your mysterious stepbrother, who you've told me nothing about."

I take a deep breath. How much to tell? "Blake starts NYU in the fall. He's a psych major. And he's . . . well, he's extremely good-looking."

Grace's mouth falls open a little. "El, do you realize how gross that sounds? He's your *family* now."

"You asked—"

"I don't care. You can't say stuff like that. It sounds like you have a crush on him."

I stare at Grace. Has she always been so contentious? It seems that ever since Jana left, Grace has transformed somehow. Maybe I'm only seeing it now that part of our trio is missing. Without Jana around to moderate our friendship, Grace and I seem more dysfunctional.

"Whatever." I need the conversation to end.

She gives me a fake-cheerful wave before I turn for home.

Near dinnertime, the door to the office/Blake's room is shut. Mom insists that I set the table with the good china since it's our first dinner as a new family. Grace's reaction to my description of Blake distracts me like a jagged fingernail, and I realize I've only used two plates, two napkins, two sets of utensils. How I wish it were just me and Mom. But I grab the extra settings before she can notice my mistake.

When Stanley comes home, Blake emerges to greet him. Not wanting to seem rude, I follow Mom to the hallway, too.

"I keep forgetting you're taller than I am now." Stanley awkwardly hugs Blake, then me, then kisses Mom. It's kind of like a visiting guest instead of a family member. I'm not sure this would ever feel routine.

"Oscar!" Mom yells. In the midst of the hugging, Stanley forgot to close the door and Oscar darts out.

I rush after him. Norma, the building superintendent, frowns at him as she exits the elevator. Oscar dashes through the doors right before they close. He's an indoor cat, and if he makes it to the lobby, manages to go outside among the cars . . . The elevator sounds like it's moving down. I bolt for the stairwell, run the six flights.

"Oscar?" I call, breathless.

He's near the lobby entrance that leads to the street, with

his ears alert and his striped tail twitching. The lady that lives in the penthouse stands on the other side, fumbling for her keys.

"Wait!" She doesn't seem to hear me. I scoop Oscar up as she opens the door.

Safely in the elevator, I blink back tears. Ten more seconds and Oscar could have been killed in traffic. He purrs in my trembling arms, oblivious to his near-miss with danger.

When I return to our floor, Norma is pounding on the door at the end of our hallway. She's a short, round woman, barely five feet tall with unruly gray hair. "Mr. Wilson, turn that down!" she shouts. He probably can't hear her with his '80s music blasting. "The neighbors are complaining again!"

She turns, spots me holding Oscar. "Pets need to stay out of the common areas," she scolds.

I'm too emotional to compose an answer. I turn my back on Norma and storm inside.

"Curiosity didn't kill the cat?" Blake says.

"No, but your father almost did." I make sure the door closes firmly behind me.

"I had no idea he would run out," Stanley says.

I'm tempted to unleash a torrent of anger when Mom puts her hand on my shoulder.

"It was an accident," she says.

I retreat to my room with Oscar. He's okay. That's all that matters. Oscar is safe. I hold him for a long time with my eyes closed. My heart barely stops racing before Mom announces that dinner's ready.

For years, Mom and I sat in our same two chairs, perpendicular to each other. I take my usual place before Blake can claim it.

"Was I in your seat this morning?" he asks, sitting across from me.

I set my jaw. "Yes." Forget the stepfamily fake-niceness.

Mom gives me her displeased look. "Ella's a creature of habit. You can sit anywhere you want."

"No, I'm the same way," he says. "I understand. This will be my new seat from now on."

It's quiet as Mom passes the pasta and her homemade marinara sauce with vegan cheese sprinkles for me and a separate bowl of sausage for everyone else. I'm not inclined to start a stupid conversation. We eat in a silent bubble of awkwardness until Stanley compliments the sauce. "Delicious," he says. "And I don't remember seeing these plates before."

"They're the good dishes," Mom says, "since it's a special occasion."

Even in my anger, I cringe. I'm not sure what the etiquette is when a father and son attempt to reconcile as part of a newly combined family. But I'm pretty sure you don't draw attention to it with the dishware. What's next—party hats and balloons?

"Everything is so nice," Blake says. Something in his

tone—envy?—makes me think he's eaten off his share of plastic plates.

"We've had these forever," I say. "They were a gift from—"

"Did you have a nice time with Grace?" Mom interrupts. I guess she doesn't want me to mention her dead husband's mother tonight.

"Yes." I can't talk about the Tarot reading. Mom is even more of a skeptic than Grace.

"What did you guys do today?" Mom asks Blake.

"We had lunch at Arthur's Tavern."

Normally, I would chime in about the restaurant's haunted bathroom, but I don't see that going over well. Our dinner conversation is surprisingly complicated.

"Good steak?" Mom asks.

"The best," Stanley says. "Blake and I had a lot of catching up to do. We spent the whole day talking. And he wanted to know all about you, and Ella, even the cat. His new family!"

I'm thinking of a cutting response when I catch Blake's exaggerated eye roll. I stifle a giggle. He must realize, too, that Mom and Stanley are acting weird. What is wrong with them? Blake's arrival has them totally off-kilter. I imagine we're part of some reality show about newly formed families. I'm tempted to glance around to search for hidden cameras.

"What's everyone doing tomorrow?" Stanley asks.

"I have to run some wedding errands," Mom says. "Ella, you'll cover the afternoon?"

I nod. I've worked every Thursday all summer, so it's an annoyingly rhetorical question.

"I'd love to see the store," Blake says. "What time are you working?"

"Eleven to four," I say in unison with Mom. It breaks the tension, and we both laugh.

From under my chair, Oscar gives a hungry meow. "I'll feed you in a few minutes."

"How was volunteering? I told Blake how you get lots of cats adopted," Stanley says. "I know you were worried about that one black cat named Flower."

"Petals," I correct him. "I didn't volunteer today." I'm not taking the bait to make cat-related conversation after he endangered Oscar's life. "When does school start?" I ask Blake.

"I move into the dorm on the twenty-fifth."

"Have you always wanted to study psychology?" Mom asks.

"Yes. It's a great program. I'm more interested in the research angle than, say, counseling."

I busy myself by twirling my spaghetti around the fork. I used to meet with a psychologist after I had anxiety issues during middle school, but I haven't needed to see her for years.

"I even got permission to take a clinical lab course spring semester of my freshman year," he continues.

"That's wonderful. I'm so happy you'll be at a school nearby." Mom beams at him, completely sucking up.

"What about you, El?" Blake asks. "Have you thought about college?"

"I want to study to be a vet. Like my dad."

Blake nods and I get the feeling he knew this already, that Stanley covered it in his afternoon discussion of all-things-Benton. I manage to change the conversation by asking him more about his upcoming classes.

After dinner, I stack some of the plates, relieved the meal is over. Blake helps by carrying a pile to the sink. It's a nice gesture, like he's stepping into his role as the dutiful son, and I'm not sure if I love him or hate him for it.

"Thank you, Blake," Mom says. "How thoughtful of you."

I load the dishwasher, which apparently isn't praiseworthy. I'm halfway done when Blake drops a plate into the sink. He reaches for it and yelps. Shards glisten among the dirty dishes. I scoop up Oscar in case fragments made it to the floor.

Blake pushes against the fleshy part of his palm with a paper towel. The resulting red spot grows larger.

"Are you okay?" I ask.

He nods, but his pale grimace says pain, even to someone who's only known him a day.

Mom frowns at the injury but her eyes look distant, confused. If she's angry about losing one of the plates, she doesn't say anything.

"How did that happen?" Stanley moves to his side. "Let me see."

"It's fine."

"Looks like you need stitches," Stanley says. "Do you want to wait here while I get the car? The parking garage is three blocks away."

"I can walk with you." Blake looks at my mom. "Will you come, too, Andrea?" He asks quietly, as if she might say no. This whole combined-family thing must be as weird to him as it is to me.

"Of course," Mom says. She looks pleased that he asked. I wouldn't invite Stanley along if I were hurt. Blake is certainly getting the better deal in the new stepparent department.

"I'll stay here and clean up," I say, still clutching Oscar.

No one answers me.

Once the plan is decided, a mini-whirlwind follows: the finding of car keys, shoes, "bring water and something to read, honey," then the door closes behind them. After I put Oscar in my bedroom out of the way, I start to sweep, but the glass seems contained in the sink. I carefully throw the biggest pieces into the trash, feeling bitter for a moment. I hope they appreciate my efforts. At least Oscar can safely roam free.

I'm relieved when the kitchen is back in order. Mom kids that I came out of the womb and asked the doctor to please tidy up. It's a dumb joke. I think my neatness gives her a certain pride (look at my daughter who keeps her room clean without asking!) and that probably reinforced my behavior over the years. I'm sure Blake could analyze the psychology behind it.

When they finally return, Blake sports a bandage and

they're laughing about the clumsy doctor. I guess it's the kind of joke you had to be there to find funny.

I've had enough family for tonight. Oscar follows me to my room. "We have to adjust," I tell him. "Blake won't be here long."

Oscar has knocked a book off my nightstand, which he does about once a week. This time it's the memoir Stanley gave me about a bitter old man whose life is transformed by adopting a cat. Mom obviously picked the book out for him to give me. He couldn't have bought such a thoughtful gift on his own, and the irony of the grumpy man was obviously lost on him.

The book has fallen open, face down. I glance at the page where it's landed, sucking in my breath when I spot the page number. Eighty-eight. My lucky number repeated twice.

# 5

# THE BET

What are the odds of my book landing open to page eighty-eight? Eight, my lucky number, always makes me think of Dad. I shiver at the coincidence. Then, after closing my bedroom door, I dig out the mini-album of Dad photos from the hiding place only Grace knows about: a tampon box on a shelf inside my closet. It's next to a package of sanitary pads so it doesn't look obvious. Grace did the same thing to keep her diary secret and it's been mom-proof for years.

The first page of the album, where my favorite photo of Dad used to be, is empty. I search the closet and finally find the photo tucked in a back corner. Did it fall out last time I looked through the album? Or did Mom go through my things? Both seem unlikely. I know Grace would totally make fun of me, but I can't help wondering if maybe it's a sign from Dad. First the book lands on the eights, then I find his photo. But that's ridiculous, right? After sliding Dad's picture back into place, I bury the tampon box inside a bin of winter sweaters for good measure.

In theory, I could have asked Mom for the photos I took. But she doesn't appreciate my connection to Dad. She didn't even believe me when Dad's spirit saved me.

It was on my eighth birthday and Mom had surprised me by saying we could get ice cream before dinner. Bouncy and excited as the two of us walked to the ice cream place, I wasn't paying attention to much except the flavors that ran through my mind. Cookie dough, strawberry banana, rainbow sherbet. I loved them all, but was leaning toward the sherbet. We were a block away from the shop when a man's voice shouted, "Ariella, wait!"

No one called me by my full name, the one Dad chose for me before he died. I froze on the spot.

Mom looked at me, impatient. "Let's go," she said, taking my hand.

"Daddy said to wait."

She was still staring at me, perplexed, when a car careened onto the sidewalk. It crashed right where we would have been walking. The driver had suffered a heart attack and lost control, but because of Dad, we stayed out of his way.

Dad kept us safe, I explained to Mom.

She rationalized that I must have fantasized Dad's voice, imagined his warning. I stole the photos from her album the next day. When I became old enough to walk to the cemetery alone, I didn't need to rely on her to take me. She's never told me outright not to go so frequently, but she gets a pained expression if I mention it.

Now, I reread the section that the book opened to. It's about black cats, how they're often considered unlucky, even evil, and therefore abused. Around Halloween, disturbed people can use superstitions as a reason to torment them. The page goes on to talk about violence against animals in general and how it can be a sign of psychological problems.

In October, the Hoboken shelter doesn't allow the adoption of black cats for fear they'll be mistreated. My favorite cat there is an older black one named Petals. She's having a hard time getting adopted. I think about stepping up my efforts to find her a home when I volunteer next week. A cute photo on the shelter's social media sites might help. But that hadn't been enough in the past.

Thoughts of Dad, mistreated cats, and ways to get Petals adopted swirl through my mind until I fall asleep.

On Thursday, I snooze the alarm twice before getting out of bed for work. I start to dress in my FREEDOM ROCKS shirt with the cat and the American flag, but I hear Grace's critical voice in my head and decide to wear a button-down blue top with black shorts and cute sandals.

Blake and I leave for the bookstore after breakfast. "I was thinking," he says as we walk there, "that we should get your mom a wedding present from the two of us. Do you have any ideas?"

I shrug. I had planned on taking a lot of photos during the

wedding, then creating an album for when they came home from Paris. The real photographer would probably make them wait weeks for the images. But I don't need Blake's help taking pictures. What else could we give Mom? "She needs a new purse, but that's hardly special enough for a wedding. Maybe a nice frame? And what about a gift for your dad, too?" I ask.

"I've got him taken care of. Wait! Does your mom have the old, new, borrowed, blue thing covered? She seems like she would appreciate the tradition."

"Hmm. She's wearing an antique clip in her hair. The dress is new. She mentioned borrowing my silver shoes. But I don't know about anything blue."

"Excellent! Then we have our mission for tomorrow. We'll go to the mall and buy her something blue. Maybe jewelry?"

"Sounds good." I try to keep my tone neutral. I'm impressed that Blake is giving her gift this much attention, but shouldn't I be the one with the awesome idea? I guess I should be thankful it will be from both of us. Maybe he's more thoughtful than I realized.

He checks his phone while we walk, then tucks it into his pocket when we arrive. I try to see the bookstore through Blake's eyes. Benton Books is on the ground floor of a brick building nestled between Manicure Mania and a trendy fitness center on Newark Street. It's an old-fashioned family kind of store, with a few comfy chairs and a children's nook with a tot-sized picnic table for kids to sit and read.

There aren't any customers in the store. Mom purposely planned her wedding and honeymoon for a slow time of year. We'll be open for limited hours with reduced staff while she's gone, so the employees get a vacation, too.

Except for Henry. He's always cranky toward me and could use the vacation more than anyone else, in my opinion. Retired and now on a second career as the assistant manager, he's my grandfather's cousin on Dad's side of the family, and he doesn't like me for some reason. Whenever I arrive, he gathers his cardigan and moves into the back room to process returns. Mom raves about him, how responsible and efficient he is, but I suspect he keeps busy to avoid me.

I introduce Blake to him but we don't chitchat. If he notices Henry's aloofness, he doesn't mention it.

"Can I help with anything?" Blake asks after I show him around.

"Not really. You should probably be careful with the stitches in your hand anyway." Still, it's nice that he offers.

He grabs the latest *Psychology Today* and relaxes in one of the chairs with his feet stretched out in front of him. I leave him there while I sort through mail on the front counter. When he's not paying attention, I skim through some books about true ghostly encounters. I can't find anything about ghosts being able to move photographs, but I do find some stories about other objects changing places.

An hour later, the door jingles and a guy about my age, maybe a year older, walks in. He's got dark spiky hair tinged a deep blue and his T-shirt sleeve doesn't quite cover the tattoo on his bicep, a swirly symmetrical shape. The bit on his muscular arm that's visible makes me curious to see the rest of it.

I straighten some papers at the register, planning to give him a few minutes to look on his own, but he comes right to the counter.

"Hey." His eyes are deep blue like his hair.

"Can I help you?" I ask.

"I'm looking for a book on cats."

"Really?" My incredulousness sounds borderline rude. "I mean, a novel or nonfiction—"

"A pet guide," he says.

"Okay, follow me." I glance around for Blake but his chair is empty. I lead the blue-haired guy to the nonfiction section and pull out three cat books. "This one is the best on behavior, this is a good health reference, and the last one captures cat-owning philosophy."

"Philosophy?"

"You know that owning a cat is way different than a dog or a hamster, right?"

"Right," he says earnestly. He takes all three to the register and pays cash.

I worry that I sounded condescending. He seems like a nice enough guy, so I try to draw the conversation out. "Did you recently adopt a cat?"

"Not yet. I thought I'd go to the shelter next week."

The mention of the shelter perks me up. "The Hoboken

shelter? I volunteer there. If you come by on Monday, I can introduce you."

"To the shelter manager?"

I grin. "No, to the cats. I should be in the cattery after twelve."

"Great." He smiles. His teeth are very white, but one tooth on the top is crooked in an adorable way. He either threw his retainers away or never had braces. "I'm Gavin," he says.

"Ella," I say. "There are kittens, of course, but if you don't mind older cats, the shelter has some sweet ones."

"Thanks." He takes the bag of books. "See you next week."

I watch him stroll out. It's a confident walk. Purposeful, but not quite a swagger.

"What am I thinking? He's so not my type."

"Who?" Blake asks.

I jump, startled. He's quieter than a slinky stray. "This guy who might adopt a cat."

"Isn't any animal lover your type?"

"With a tattoo and blue hair? Mom would think he looks dangerous. I'm not even sure Grace would approve."

"How many boyfriends have you had?"

I cross my arms. "Plenty."

I don't need to tell him that there's only been two and a half. Collin and I broke up when he realized, after every date made him wheeze, that he was allergic to Oscar. I dated another shelter volunteer, but his family moved to North Carolina and we lost touch. And I went out with Jordan, who adored me, but I didn't feel the same about him and we only lasted two weeks. I figure that counted as a partial boyfriend experience.

"Maybe you need to date someone from outside your usual social circle," Blake says. "You need to broaden your horizons, to use the cliché."

"Blake, you realize he's adopting a cat, not asking me out."

"He hasn't asked you on a date *yet*. I bet he will."

"Right. You didn't even meet him," I say. "How can you know that?"

"You look nice today."

"Gee, thanks. Isn't that a bit superficial?"

"No, when you look good, you act more confident. It's basic psychology," he says. "Want to make a bet? Twenty dollars says he asks you out. Within a week."

I frown. "Twenty is a lot."

"You must not be sure, then."

I take the bet and hope that Gavin doesn't show up at the shelter next week. Sort of. It might be nice if he did.

The rest of the afternoon shift is uneventful. On the way home, Blake and I split up, and I stop to visit Grace at work. She takes a break and sits outside with me.

"I have such a headache. I think I hate kids," she says. "Next summer, I'll get a job someplace else."

"Like a coffee shop?" Grace is practically addicted to caffeine. I only drink it once in a while. I went through a diet soda phase and learned that excessive caffeine and anxiety don't go well together.

"Or a movie theater," she says. "I bet when it's not busy I could watch movies for free." Grace loves movies even more than coffee.

"Or a movie theater next to a coffee shop. Then you'd cover all your favorites."

"I can dream about it." She sighs. "For now, I need to go back inside and face the little monsters."

"Hey, wait. I wanted to ask you. Did anyone ever find your hiding spot?"

"The tampon box?"

I nod.

"Yeah, Piper found it at the beginning of the summer. I'm asking for a doorknob that locks for my birthday. Why?"

"It's nothing," I say.

"Grace!" her manager calls.

I'm relieved that I don't need to tell her about the moving photo and the falling book. It would give her something else to tease me about.


After dinner, Stanley sets up chess in the living room for him and Blake. When we've all finished cleaning the kitchen, Mom sits on one end of the couch with her book and I sit at the other while Stanley and Blake play.

"When you're in Paris, you have to visit the Louvre and look for a chess set on display from the Middle Ages," Blake says. "The board is made of crystal and smoked quartz squares with silver edges. It's amazing. I've seen pictures online."

"We'll add the chess set to our list of must-sees," Mom says. Stanley is frowning—about to lose, I suspect.

Oscar jumps onto my lap. "Hey, old man."

"He seems very attached to you," Blake says, still waiting for Stanley to make a move.

"My dad rescued him as a kitten, so he's lived with us since right before I was born. He's going on sixteen now, the same as me."

"Oh, I thought . . . Dad, didn't you say—"

Stanley gives Blake a death-stare, one of his frowns on steroids. Mom scrutinizes the page she's reading as if it's incredibly fascinating.

"Never mind." Blake focuses on the game, avoiding my eyes. "I just thought Oscar was younger."

There's something weird happening that I can't quite figure out. It's like a favorite knick-knack out of place after Mom gets her biannual urge to dust my room.

"Mom? What's going on?"

"It's a long story."

"We have plenty of time to talk."

"Okay." She gently shuts her book. "I guess I should finally tell you. Oscar is, well, he's really Oscar the Second."

"What do you mean?"

"Remember when you and I were going to Disney World? And Oscar got sick right before we left?"

"Yeah. So?"

"Well, he never recovered. The vet tried everything, but he passed away the night before the trip. It would have broken your five-year-old heart. As soon as we got back, I adopted a cat that looked like Oscar. Of course, his coloring was slightly different, and his size. You thought he had lost weight and acted strange because he missed us. It was an adjustment, but soon the new Oscar was part of our family and you loved him just the same."

"Oscar the Second." I try to comprehend the trick Mom's played on me for most of my life. Oscar was my living connection to Dad. I fight back the tears.

"I'm sorry. But we did give a shelter cat a good life," she says, as if that excuses the deceit.

Stanley takes forever to move a piece. I can feel Blake's eyes on me, but I won't meet his gaze.

I wait several minutes before going to my room with Oscar so that it's not completely obvious that I'm having an inner tantrum. Once I'm there, I'm trapped. I slam dresser drawers, punch my pillow a few times, jerk the closet door open. Nothing makes me feel less angry. I check on my photo of Dad. It's still hidden.

"I can't believe she lied," I whisper, closing the box.

Restless, I look for something to tidy up. It's one of my coping mechanisms, a way to reduce stress. I might not be able to control everything in life, but at least I can impose order on my bedroom. I decide to reorganize my closet as a distraction. Grace's sister, Piper, might like some of the clothes I don't wear anymore, even if they're just to sleep in, so I make a bag for her. I bet she'll appreciate it, because Grace would rather throw things out than give them to Piper. It makes me feel slightly better to think about someone else's dysfunctional family.

Oscar rests on my bed as I clean. "I still love you," I tell him. "Even if you are the Oscar-replacement. The good news is we'll have more years together than I thought."

Mom calls to me from her room when I finally emerge. She's packing for the honeymoon, rolling up each outfit to maximize the space. "Want to help me?" she asks. "Or at least keep me company?"

I'm still miffed about the Oscar lie, so I stall. I compare the pile on her bed to the space in her suitcase. "Is it all going to fit?"

"I hope so. Six nights away is overwhelming. I haven't been on a trip this long since . . . since Disney." She pauses. "About Oscar. I'm sorry I didn't tell you sooner. At first, you were too young, and I didn't want to upset you. Then, as you got older, you were so comfortable with the second Oscar. It would have been disruptive to tell you the truth and it almost seemed pointless. I'm sorry for not being honest."

"Hmmph." I'm glad she apologized, but I don't want to let her off that easy for a decade of lying. She hands me a bundled pair of gray pants and I squish them on the side of the suitcase. We work wordlessly for a few minutes. She rolls. I stuff.

"It's just that Oscar was a link to Dad. It was his last gift to us." I pause. "You know your old photos of Dad? I took some to keep in my room." I know this will irk her, but she won't fight me tonight after her Oscar deceit was revealed.

Her hesitation is barely noticeable. "All you have to do is ask, honey. You can have any of the photos you want."

"Great. Thanks."

She hands me a white skirt with embroidered flowers, each petal stitched in black thread. I stare at the black flowers.

"You don't like that one?" she asks.

"It's pretty. I was just wondering. Does anyone ever visit Dad at the cemetery?"

"Not that I know of. Why would you bring that up?"

"There were flowers by his tombstone."

"Oh." She presses her lips together, handing me a rolled sweater. "So, how are you and Blake getting along?"

I'm surprised at her change of subject, but she seems determined not to get into another argument with me.

"Fine. He asked if I would do errands with him tomorrow."

"That's good. It will give you a chance to get to know each other." She passes me a short-sleeved black top. "You know you're still the most important person to me."

She's said this before, but I'm not tired of hearing it. "I know. Thank you."

"No more Two Musketeers." Her voice is bittersweet.

"Blake would have to analyze the psychology of musketeers before joining," I joke.

"I'm glad you're becoming friends. It makes me feel better about leaving. By the way, I've put Henry in charge of running the bookstore while I'm away. Maybe you can check on him occasionally?"

"Sure." Henry would not welcome any interference from me. But I don't want Mom to worry about business on her honeymoon.

She closes the suitcase, then pushes on the center as I zip it from the sides.

"I have a bit more to pack but at least I know this stuff fits. You're still okay with me going, right? I'll leave you some spending money. And I spoke to Grace's mom. Staying there from Sunday night onward works with their schedule, too. They're happy to have you."

The six nights would undoubtedly be filled with lots of movie-watching. Grace might not believe in the supernatural, but she loves all kinds of scary movies.

"I bet you won't even miss us," Mom says.

# 6

# VÉRITÉ

Skyler, the shelter manager, calls Friday morning after breakfast. A pipe burst at the Jersey City shelter and some of the dogs and cats will be relocated to our facility in Hoboken. "We need to get ready for the new animals," she says. "Any chance you can come in for a few hours?"

I arrive a half hour later, sign in, and stride toward cattery number one. Despite the faint disinfectant smell, I love this place. Sixteen healthy cats currently call the room home. Carpeted cat trees and scratching posts are scattered throughout the center for playtime. Wire cages line two of the walls and under the window is a shelf with cat beds built into it. Curled in the middle bed, Petals snoozes in the sun.

I say hello to her before I do anything else. She's a beautiful old cat with black fur and greenish eyes. She leans into my hand as I rub behind her ears.

"Maybe today will be your lucky day, Petals."

Skyler joins me in the cattery. "You love that cat so much. Why don't you adopt her?"

"I wish I could. Our building has a one-pet rule," I say. "What's our mission for this afternoon?"

She pushes her blonde, wavy hair behind her ears. "We need to move more of our animals out quickly to make room for the Jersey City ones, so the adoption fees will be temporarily waived. We're also going to have a Shelter Beach Party–themed week starting on Monday. I've picked up some beach balls, floppy sun hats, and other decorations. What do you think?"

I think the cats might puncture the beach balls, but I don't want to be negative. "Sounds good. We should update the animal photos on the website to match the theme."

"I'll get the camera," she says.

We spend most of the morning trying to pose cats with beach props, which is a lot harder than I imagined. We succeed in surrounding Petals with fake flowers for her photo, not exactly beach-themed, but still adorable, given her name. It makes me remember, for a moment, the black flowers at Dad's grave. I shake off the unpleasant thoughts and focus on the next picture.

When we finish with the cats, I wish her luck with the dog photos and head home. While I'm walking, I decide to research the flowers at Dad's grave. They didn't look dyed, like carnations or daisies. I search for Hoboken florists using my phone, then call them all. None sell any naturally black flowers. One lady explains that black roses are actually a very dark red.

"I'm not looking specifically for roses," I explain.

"There's not a big demand for black in general," she says. "Revenge, hatred, death. Hardly a best seller."

I thank her and hang up, more confused than ever about where the flowers came from.

After a quick sandwich, Blake and I are about to leave for Mom's "blue" gift outing when she sees us by the door.

"Where are you headed?" she asks.

"Just leaving for the mall," I say, "to buy a . . ." I'm not prepared to lie. I go blank.

"A tie." Blake's voice is smooth and natural. "Ella said she'd help me pick one for the wedding."

"Wait." Mom leaves and comes back with some folded bills. "In case you see something nice." She hands me the cash. "Have fun!"

Inside the elevator, Blake chuckles. "You," he says, "are the Worst. Liar. Ever."

I shrug. "She caught me off guard." But the truth is, I hate to lie to her.

The train is empty. Blake takes a navy drawstring bag off his back and puts it on the seat between us. As the train jolts forward, I think about his excuse to Mom. "Do you still need a tie?"

"No, I bought the one you chose, remember?"

I shift in my seat, thinking about how taken aback I was by his beauty that first day. I wasn't even sure he remembered meeting me.

"You arrived on an earlier plane," I say, "but you didn't tell them. How did you know I wouldn't give you away? I could've mentioned that we'd already met."

"It didn't seem likely," he says. "I gambled that it wouldn't come up."

Where did he sleep that night? I wait for the rest of the story, but he doesn't share anything more with me.

When we near the mall, I spot the same homeless man with the German shepherd. Blake stops and opens his bag. He hands the guy several cans of dog food and some protein bars.

"God bless," the man says. "Thank you."

Wow. I'm impressed that Blake remembered him from his last trip to the mall, too, and clearly made the effort to help. Without Mom to interfere, I hand the man five dollars from the money she gave me. It starts our afternoon together on a positive note.

Inside the mall, we try a few smaller jewelry stores before ending up at Macy's. We pass by my dress, the one I wanted to wear to the wedding, and I can't help pausing to run my hand over the yellow fabric. I must sigh aloud, because Blake wants to know what's wrong.

"Nothing. Mom and I disagreed about what I should wear to the wedding, and she won."

"Yeah, Dad was pretty specific about my suit, too."

After wandering through the costume necklaces, we find a glass case of more expensive jewelry. We both see it at the same time: a bracelet with ice-blue Swarovski crystals.

"It's perfect," he says.

"Yes, she'll love it."

It doesn't feel right to use the cash Mom gave me on her own present, but I have money saved from the bookstore. We split the cost and leave happy.

"That was pretty painless," Blake says.

"Now what?" I say.

"Do you need to do any other shopping?"

"Actually, I'd love to stop in the makeup store."

"Okay. How about we meet where we came in? Does one o'clock give you enough time?" he asks.

"Yes, that's great."

Sephora isn't that busy. The store is out of my price range, but I decide to splurge with the cash from Mom. They usually require an appointment for a makeover, but I explain about the wedding tomorrow and the beauty consultant takes pity and fits me in.

Forty-five minutes later, I look like an enhanced version of me. I saunter toward the exit with a little black and white bag containing eyeliner and eye shadow, nervous about what Blake will say about my look.

*That's dumb*, I remind myself. *He's your stepbrother, not your boyfriend.*

His face lights up when he sees me. "Wow!" He moves the hair away from my face. "You look nice."

It's a small gesture, but his touch unnerves me. I need to get a grip. "Thank you."

He carries a large Macy's shopping bag, but doesn't chat about what he bought the way Jana or Grace would. They'd be pulling clothes out and showing me right there, unable to wait. I guess guys are different. I stop in the food court to buy bottled water for the homeless man, and then we head home. One more day until the wedding. We're as ready as we are going to be.

Later that night, Grace and I talk on the phone.

"What did you do today?" she asks.

"I went to the mall with Blake to buy a wedding present for my mom."

"How's everything with that hot stepbrother of yours?"

"Leave me alone. You'll get to meet him tomorrow."

"Right. Then Sunday night our sleepover extravaganza begins!"

"Yes," I say, laughing.

"Is there anything special you'd like to do, besides watch movies?"

I had thought of one thing. "Yes, but you won't like it."

"What? An evening Tarot reading?"

"Close. I was thinking maybe we could have a séance."

"Ugh."

Just the reaction I expected. "It's my dad's birthday next week."

"I don't know . . ."

"I realize nothing will happen, Grace. It will be for fun."

"Maybe. If you agree to watch—"

There's a tap on my bedroom door.

"Hold on," I tell her. I open it to find Blake, dressed in jeans and a black T-shirt.

"Let's go," he whispers.

"Where?" I mouth.

He looks at my Felix the Cat pjs. "Get dressed, and meet me in the kitchen," he whispers. "Trust me."

I close the door behind him. Where could we possibly go at this time of night? Still, my curiosity is piqued.

"Grace? Sorry." For a moment, I consider telling her I'm going out with Blake. But I'd never hear the end of it, I rationalize. "Mom's hounding me to get some sleep. We've got a big day tomorrow. You know how she is."

"Okay," she says, but she sounds disappointed that we didn't finish planning. "I'll see you tomorrow."

After we hang up, I throw on capris and my newest T-shirt, I WOULD PUSH YOU IN FRONT OF ZOMBIES TO SAVE MY CAT. The silence means Mom and Stanley are already in bed. I give Oscar a quick pet, grab my wallet, then rush to meet Blake.

We talk in whispers until we're outside in the courtyard next to our building. Blake chooses a bench that's half in the shadows, then opens a Poland Spring bottle and takes a swig that tells me it isn't filled with water. When he offers it to me, I'm feeling high on rebellion. Sneaking out is more fun than I imagined. I take a polite sip even though it smells gross. My mouth crinkles in disgust.

"Vodka tonic," he says. "I couldn't exactly hide a fruity drink in a water bottle."

I would never steal alcohol from my mom, but he doesn't seem to mind taking risks. I'm a little impressed at his boldness.

"I thought it would be good to get outside, away from Stanley and Andrea for a while." He takes another swig. The white bandage covering his stitches stands out in the dim light.

"Does your hand still hurt?" I ask.

"It's not bad. Your mom was great, by the way. She stayed totally calm. My dad, not so much."

"I've been wondering . . . you and Stanley aren't close, right?"

"Not since the divorce. My parents couldn't make it work, Mom told me. After my baby sister died, my mom grieved for a long time. My dad found it easier to be away from us, I guess. Everyone handles death in their own way. His way was to disappear."

"Oh, I'm so sorry. He didn't mention it, only that it was a difficult divorce. I had no idea that he had a daughter who died."

"The death of a child causes a major strain on a marriage. Anything difficult with a child, actually—a serious physical problem, severe mental illness, a fatal accident—it can doom a couple. I learned about it in psychology. I also learned how unhealthy it is to hold a grudge, so I eventually decided to forgive him. Now with the wedding coming up, it seemed like a good time for us to make peace." He takes another drink. "Enough about my drama. Who were you talking to when I knocked on your door?"

"Grace. We've been friends forever."

"Does she love animals, too?"

"Not exactly. She's a movie fanatic. We have an unspoken agreement. I sit through whatever she picks, and she spends occasional afternoons with me in front of the grocery store, collecting donations for the animal shelter."

"I had a gray kitten in middle school, but he disappeared. Ran away, I guess. I was so upset that I missed a week of classes."

"That's so sad. Did Stanley and your mom . . ." I try to calculate the timeline of their divorce. His parents split up way before my mom met Stanley, but I don't really know when. "I mean, did anyone put up fliers?"

"My dad had already left by then," he says matter-of-factly. He pauses. "You're probably wondering why I came to Hoboken early and didn't say anything."

I nod.

"I have a girlfriend here, so I stayed at her apartment. We met on my last trip to the East Coast."

"Oh." A girlfriend? I never considered that. If she has her own apartment, she must be older. Not anyone I would know. "Why not just tell him that?"

"Then he'd want to meet her and be all over-involved with my life. He hasn't had much to do with me for years. I don't need an insta-dad. Small steps," Blake says. "Now you know my secret."

I wonder what she looks like. Beautiful, no doubt. "I won't say anything."

"I know I can trust you." Blake smiles. "Since we're sharing secrets, I'll tell you another one. I knew it was you when I saw you at the mall. Dad had sent me a photo of the three of you, and I recognized you from the picture. I wanted to introduce myself, but I chickened out. So I asked you about the ties instead."

"That makes sense. It felt like too much of a coincidence that we'd randomly run into each other." It wasn't fate after all, like I'd thought that afternoon. It makes me sad that our meeting wasn't as destined as it seemed. "You do have good taste in ties."

"Thanks." The cool breeze cheers me. It's refreshing to sit outside on a summer night, after the oppressive heat of the daytime has lifted. I've been struggling with jealousy since Blake's arrival, but it occurs to me that the family situation is weird for him, too. I feel almost warm from the fact that he trusts me with his secrets. It's either that or the vodka.

"Let's play a game," he says. "*Deux vérités et un mensonge.* You tell me two truths and a lie, and I'll try to guess which one isn't true."

I hate this kind of thing, but I do want us to be friends, to cement this moment of closeness. "Were you speaking French?" I stall while I try to think of something interesting.

"*Oui*. My mom is Canadian. Veronique insisted that I study French," he says. "Ready to play?"

I think it over another moment. "Um, Veggie Paradise is my favorite take-out place. Pink is my favorite color. I secretly believe in ghosts."

"That's easy. There's no way pink is your favorite color."

I smile. "Right."

"Why is your belief in ghosts a secret?"

I remember the car crashing over the curb and explaining to Mom how Dad told me to wait. She looked at me like I was lying that day. Or irrational.

"Mom's pretty skeptical about that stuff. So is Grace. I try to downplay it," I say. "Now, it's your turn."

"I've never been to the Atlantic Ocean. I've always wanted a sister. I love chess."

"You're lying about the ocean?"

He laughs. "You've got it. I've been to the Jersey Shore a bunch of times. My dream is to live on an island, surrounded by the ocean. And I love chess. It brings back good memories of my dad, before the divorce. Do you play?"

"No. I understand how the pieces move but I've never been able to strategize."

"What games do you like?"

"Backgammon."

"Ah, strategy plus luck. You never know how the dice will roll." He drains the rest of the drink. "Do you want to sneak into Lana's?" He motions toward the bar across the street.

"I've got a great fake ID. I bet the bouncer would look away for a pretty girl."

*He thinks I'm pretty.* I hesitate. "Thanks, but Mom would kill me."

"She seems strict."

"It's been the two of us forever. She always wants to keep me out of trouble, especially in a bar. A drunk driver leaving a pub killed my dad."

Blake looks away as if he's deciding something.

"What?" I ask. He doesn't answer right away, but I let the silence weigh on him. It always works with Grace and Jana.

Finally, he turns to me. "You seem like the kind of person who values the truth, no matter what."

"Yes. Who doesn't?"

"You'd be surprised. Some people don't mind being deceived. They like to stay in denial. But I don't ever want to be dishonest with you."

"Dishonest about what?"

He hesitates. "I shouldn't give away your mom's secret," he says. "She confided in Stanley, and he told me. You can't let your mom know."

I jiggle my leg. All this dancing around the topic annoys me. "Fine."

"I know our parents getting married doesn't guarantee us becoming friends. But I meant what I said about wanting a sister. And I hate dishonesty, especially about something as important as your own dad."

I suddenly wish there was more vodka left in his bottle. "What about him?"

Blake meets my gaze. "He wasn't killed in a car accident."

"What? What are you talking about?"

"Your dad . . . he died in a mental hospital."

"No. No, you must be confused. It was a car accident. Mom told me."

He's silent.

"You must have misunderstood." Irritation creeps into my voice.

"I don't think so. She told Stanley about it."

As I consider it, I can hear everything nearby: glasses clinking in the bar across the street, car motors idling at the red light, cat cries in the distance. I let the sounds wash over me. What Blake said can't be true.

"Mom wouldn't lie to me for all these years." But even as I argue, Oscar the Second comes to mind. "Not about something this important. Besides, you've been out of touch with Stanley, and now all you can discuss is the secrets Mom keeps?"

"I might have probed a little," Blake says. "It's easier to talk about your family than my own."

"You're wrong about my dad."

"Am I?" Blake keeps his voice gentle. "Are you sure your mom never looked uncomfortable talking about the specifics of how he died? Did she always change the subject after telling you minimal facts about his death?"

The smallest sliver of doubt wedges its way inside. I don't know many details, except that Dad worked late to save an injured dog. Then he had a meeting, something related to vets, before a drunk driver killed him on his way home.

Blake must sense my hesitation. "All right. I didn't want to get my dad in trouble. But if it's that important and you still don't believe me, ask your mom tomorrow."

"On her wedding day? I don't think so."

"Have you read the obituary?" he asks.

"Of course." I went through a phase where I read it often, hoping to find Dad somewhere in the black and white print. I practically memorized the brief paragraphs. "It said that he died in an accident and that it was under investigation."

Blake presses his lips together, as if he's considering something.

"What?" I'm nearly shouting.

"An accident could cover a lot of situations," he says.

I work to control my voice. "Mom values her privacy. There's no way she would put the whole story in his obituary, especially when there were criminal charges against the driver." This conversation is ridiculous. I stand, ready to go home. After the honeymoon, I'll ask Mom myself. Then I'll show Blake that he is wrong.

"I wouldn't lie to you, El," he says, as if he can read my mind. "If you don't believe me, I'll figure out a way to prove it."

# 7

# FACTS

The morning sun peeks around the edges of my window shade like any other day. Then I feel the dread, the hollowness in my stomach, as I remember what Blake said about Dad.

Why does the possibility that Dad was unwell irritate me so much? It's not the mental illness itself that bothers me. Lots of people have problems and get treatment. Jana's uncle is bipolar and my US History teacher talked openly about her depression. I can't help wondering about my own anxiety. Maybe it is hereditary, something Mom could have mentioned to me, but didn't.

Oscar curls against me, and I rub his belly as he purrs. Mom lied. Again. Why come up with an elaborate story about a drunk driver? She could have gone with a simple fib, like a heart attack. And she didn't need to lie at all when I became old enough to understand. The really bothersome part is that she would tell the truth to Stanley and not to me. Mom and I are always honest with each other. Or so I believed.

Her one big lie makes all my smaller images of Dad feel false. What if he actually hated the color yellow? What if he didn't even paint my room? My carefully constructed world-of-Dad feels like a sandcastle.

No. Blake must be wrong. I feel it in my gut. Propped against my pillows, I use my laptop to search for new information to counter what Blake said. I find the obituary for Thomas Darren Benton, a popular Hoboken veterinarian who died suddenly. I've read it a gazillion times before. I always assumed the cause of death was vague because Mom's a private kind of person or because the legal case against the man who killed him was still pending.

The Internet offers nothing new. I close the laptop with more force than necessary. The apartment seems quiet. I find myself hoping I'm alone with Mom. Wedding day or not, maybe I could figure out a way to ask her about Dad.

No such luck. I find Blake at the kitchen table in an NYU T-shirt, drinking his coffee. Oscar follows me and figure-eights my legs.

"Andrea went with my dad to pick up his suit from the tailor," he says. "They were giddy with excitement."

"Uh-huh." I open cat food, plop the mush into the metal bowl. Oscar devours it in his usual ravenous style.

"You ready for today?" Blake asks.

"Mmm."

"You're angry with me, aren't you? I'm sorry for last night.

My timing sucks. But I'm not a liar. You deserve to know the truth. What if I could provide evidence? Would that put your mind at ease?"

Without answering, I fall into the kitchen chair like Alice down the rabbit hole.

He pours a cup of coffee with one sugar, slides it toward me as he sits. I wonder how he remembers that's how I like it. It's thoughtful of him, and it softens my mood a little.

"What's your idea?" I ask.

He leans toward me, his eyes serious. "We should contact the closest hospitals, the ones he most likely stayed at. I searched online and found three. You can call and say you want a copy of his records. There must be something about his death on file."

I sigh, staring at the calendar on the kitchen bulletin board. Mom marked today, August 6, "WEDDING" in her loopy handwriting. The box for August 8, Dad's birthday, remains empty. His death date, August 30, is also blank, not that I would expect her to note it on the calendar.

"We have enough time before they get back," Blake says. "Do you want to call now?"

"Not really." The situation is absurd, but maybe if there are no records he'll be forced to drop the whole idea.

He hands me a printout of the hospital addresses and numbers. I enter the numbers slowly, thankful when I get put on hold after pressing six for "other information" from the automated menu. When a woman answers, I explain that I'd like copies of my father's records. "Can you please send them to me?"

"I'm sorry, but that's against our privacy policy. Only someone designated as the patient's personal representative can access them."

"But—"

"Those are the rules."

"Can you at least confirm that the records exist?"

"I can't help you without proper authorization."

When I hang up, Blake is eager for a recap. I explain what the woman said. The next two calls go the same way. "I guess I'll ask Mom after the honeymoon." I hold the warm mug between both hands.

"There has to be a way around it." Blake pours himself more coffee. "Who would have been your dad's personal representative? Your mom?"

"I have no idea." I don't want to play this guessing game. "Maybe a lawyer. Why do you care so much about this?"

"It bothers me that you don't believe me. Deep down, don't you want to know?"

He interprets my silence as a yes. I'd prefer to keep my previous beliefs about Dad a little while longer, even if they're wrong.

But Blake is on a roll. "We have to make the request from a lawyer. Or me, impersonating a lawyer. Which of these hospitals is closest?"

I point to Meadowview Psychiatric on the list. "But we don't even know if this would be the right hospital. I don't see—"

"Let's give it a try. It'll only take a few minutes," he says. "Look, I can do this better if you're not listening. It makes me self-conscious."

Taking the phone into his bedroom, he closes the door. From my closet, I bet I can hear every word. I push the bin of winter sweaters out of the way and sit on the floor under my hanging clothes, close enough to the wall to listen.

Blake says he's the family lawyer and that the insurance company is requesting the information about my father. Of course, he realizes it's been sixteen years. How should he know why? Insurance companies are always difficult and he needs the records ASAP. Yes, even if they are in the archives. Yes, a summary would be fine instead of the whole file. Yes, he'll fax a written request.

It's quite a performance and despite my reluctance I can't help but admire Blake. If only it weren't all happening so fast. I take some deep breaths, delay leaving my room. I don't really want proof of Mom's deception—especially not today.

Blake's already creating a fake lawyer letterhead when I scramble out of my closet and find him in the kitchen. "What's Andrea's date of birth?" he asks.

I rattle it off as he types, prints, signs. Then he faxes it from his room.

My stomach rumbles, and whether it's nerves or hunger, I decide a bowl of cereal with rice milk will help. "Want some?"

Blake waves away my offer and microwaves his coffee-gone-cold.

"She said Saturdays are slow, that she can send it within the hour," he says.

He got a much nicer lady on the phone than the one I spoke to. I'm not sure I want the machine to churn out the answer to whether or not my mother has lied to me my entire life. As I'm mulling this over, the key turns in the door.

*Oh no.* Blake and I look at each other, and I'm sure his panicked expression mirrors my own. The ringer on the fax is always off, but the machine will beep loudly once the transmission is complete.

Mom and Stanley come in, bubbly and joyful. They describe their morning in great detail, telling us about the flowers and the suit and the optimistic weather forecast. I can barely focus.

"It's a beautiful day!" Mom says.

When she pauses in her monologue, the crinkly noise of paper being faxed is so loud I think for sure she'll investigate. But she launches into the reception decorations instead. Blake excuses himself, scraping his chair as he gets up from the table. His bedroom door clicks closed.

Did we pull it off? Growing up alone, I never had a real partner in crime. I'm almost gleeful until I realize what the records signify. This can't be good.

Meanwhile, Mom explains our schedule for the photographer and the reception.

"I better get ready." I put my dishes in the dishwasher. When she isn't paying attention, I dart down the hallway into Blake's room.

He holds out several pages. "Proof."

I would rather clean the litter box with my bare hands than take them. I do it anyway, skimming enough to realize that my father was actually a patient at Meadowview.

PATIENT NAME: THOMAS DARREN BENTON
PATIENT NUMBER: 47625

I still can't believe it. "Why wouldn't Mom tell me the truth?"

"The psychology of a lie." Blake rubs between his eyes. "At first maybe it was too hard to explain. Later, it probably became so ingrained, such a part of the history you believed, she couldn't figure out how to unwind it."

Isn't that what she said about Oscar?

"Maybe you're right." I take the papers and tuck them under my shirt. In the safety of my room, with one hand on Oscar for comfort, I read the documents that make me question the foundation Mom raised me on.

Dad.

Depression.

Accidental overdose.

The magnitude of the past ripples into my present. I don't know Dad nearly as well as I thought I did.

Then there's Mom, the only person who's been there for my entire existence. She's the constant in a life of variables.

Apparently, I don't know her that well, either.

# 8

# GIFTS

As I get ready for the wedding, I try to process everything new I've learned about Dad. It's like someone ripped out part of *To Kill a Mockingbird* and replaced it with pages from *The Catcher in the Rye*. It makes zero sense. I can't reconcile my hero dad with someone sad and depressed.

It's from Dad that I got my love of cats, my left-handedness, and my need for order. We're connected through these little details. Even though he didn't help raise me, I considered him part of my life, part of my history.

Does knowing how he died change any of that? I had imagined a compassionate Dad dying, indirectly, because of his commitment to animals. He had stayed late the night he was killed. Now I have to rewrite the legend in my mind.

I need to focus on the wedding. I've straightened my frizzy hair but the eye shadow that made me so confident yesterday isn't working any magic today. I'm running out of time. Close to tears, I call Grace and beg her to come over.

"What's the matter?" she says when we're alone in my room.

"I can't do this." I wave my hand over the makeup lined up across my dresser.

"Okay." She takes stock of the situation. "Your hair looks nice. If you put the mascara on, I can do everything else. Is it waterproof?"

I nod.

"Good. Because you look like you might cry any minute. Should I tell you about my latest favorite villain to distract you?"

"No horror movies now, Grace." But I can't help smiling. She finishes my makeup and it looks almost as good as it did in the store. Now I just need to change out of my pjs.

Blake shows up at my door, looking like a model in his gray suit along with the tie I picked. Grace sucks in her breath.

"Grace, this is my stepbrother, Blake. Blake, this is my friend, Grace."

"Hey," he says, flashing her a smile. He hands me a shopping bag. "We're supposed to meet the photographer in half an hour. I hope this didn't get too wrinkled."

I take it from him. Inside is a longer plastic bag around a hanger. I slip off the plastic and gasp.

It's the glamorous yellow dress, the one I really wanted.

"Surprise," Blake says. "After you mentioned it at the mall, I thought maybe it would make you happy."

"Wow! How did you—"

"I went back when you were in Sephora. I guessed at the size."

"El, it's beautiful," Grace says.

I lay the dress across my bed.

"But Mom will have a fit! This is the one she picked." I pull out the ruffled-rose thing and hold it against me.

Grace makes a face like Oscar threw up a hairball.

"It's bad, isn't it?" I ask.

"I should stay out of this," Blake says. "Grace, what do you think?"

"The yellow one is so much prettier."

I frown. It's Mom's special day. Then again, I'm not feeling all that accommodating after learning about her lies.

"It was really nice of you to buy this for me, and it's the perfect size. I'll be ready in a few minutes," I tell Blake.

"I'll wait with him in the kitchen while you change," Grace says.

They leave me alone in my room, and I shut the door behind them. The entire back of my bedroom door is covered with a giant cat collage and I run my hand over a few of the images. I remember carefully selecting the pictures and arranging them by their expressions one by one. Cheerful cats, sad cats, mischievous cats. Even though they aren't precisely lined up, something about the collage has always made me happy. Mom, to her credit, didn't complain about the three rolls of tape the project required.

I have to stop stalling and get ready. Choosing a dress

shouldn't be so hard. "This is crazy," I mumble. But the word *crazy* makes me think of Dad and mental illness. I shake off my own words and select a dress.

When I finally emerge, Grace has gone home. Blake and Stanley have left to meet the photographer. Mom's in the kitchen alone, jingling her keys.

She smiles as she checks out my rose-colored glory. "You look beautiful."

"So do you." She's wearing a white lace dress that comes to her knees. "Are you nervous?"

"A happy nervous," she says. "How are you?"

It's my chance to ask about Dad. "Um, Blake mentioned . . ." But how can I do this now? What if she becomes emotional right before the photographs? "He said he had a sister who died at birth. Why didn't Stanley tell me when we spoke about the divorce?"

Mom sighs. "Even after all these years, it's hard for him to discuss. Death can be like that."

*Yes. Death can be like that.*

She glances at the clock. "We shouldn't be late."

"No, of course not."

We meet Ken, the photographer, at the park next to our building. The Hudson River sparkles in the sunshine. Stanley can't stop smiling.

"Everyone looks gorgeous," he says.

Blake glances at me, then looks away. I was so worried

about Mom's reaction to the yellow dress that it never occurred to me that he would be hurt if I didn't choose it.

While Ken and his assistant set up, I stand next to Blake.

"The dress . . . it was really nice of you. But I didn't want to upset her today."

"Of course. Save it for another special occasion." He hands me the bracelet box. His stitches are covered with a small adhesive bandage instead of the bulky white gauze. "We should give it to her now."

I nod. "Mom, Blake and I have a wedding present for you."

"Oh, how sweet!" She opens the box. "It's beautiful. And the blue. How thoughtful." She hugs Blake, then me, quick enough that she can't feel me stiffen, but not before I see her eyes tear.

"It was all Ella's idea," he says.

"No, actually—"

Ken claps his hands. "Let's go, folks."

The photography madness begins. He arranges us in different family combinations. Me and Mom. Blake and Stanley. Me and Blake. The four of us. It goes on and on.

When I'm not in the shot, I use my own camera to photograph his poses. My plan is still to make an album as a wedding present so they'll have photos right after the honeymoon. I also bought a book for Stanley about the history of chess that I snuck into his suitcase as a surprise.

I watch Mom smile for the camera and push her lie out of my mind, not wanting it to taint the day. Still, I have to try not to pull away when I pose with her, as if something has shifted, a crack in our family veneer.

As the photographer packs up his lenses, a white limousine pulls up to the park. Mom looks at Stanley, but he's as puzzled as she is.

"Nice ride, huh?" Blake links his arm through mine. "This is our present to you, Dad."

I feel my mouth drop and make an effort to look normal.

"You've got it until midnight," Blake explains. "Then it turns into a VW beetle."

"Well, it sure beats a taxi," Stanley says.

"What a lovely treat!" Mom says as the driver holds the door open for her. "You two are full of surprises."

I try to catch Blake's eye before we enter the limo but I can't. His present is a good idea, a great one, actually. I wish he'd told me everything he planned. Now I owe him for the dress, the limo, and the truth.

# 9

# VOWS

The reception takes place on the second floor of The Brass Rail. The restaurant is one of Hoboken's haunted places, but that didn't dissuade Mom from choosing it. White tulle wraps the railing of the grand staircase and the upstairs room is decorated in black and white. I'm relieved to see white lilies at the center of each table. For the briefest moment, I imagine them replaced by the black flowers at Dad's grave.

The party is a small affair: Lisa, Mom's friend who first introduced her to Stanley; Stanley's brother and his family of four; Lucille, who works at the bookstore, and grumpy Henry, too; some guy named Mike who's known Stanley since they were young; a few other random family and friends. Jana is still away, but Grace, Piper, and their parents, Mr. and Mrs. Wallace, are here.

The whole evening passes quickly, almost like flipping through a series of photos: the four of us taking the limo ride to the restaurant. The I-dos. Mom and Stanley dancing to some mushy, old-fashioned song on the temporary dance floor. Stanley saying, "It's nice to have you as a daughter, Ella. Call me if you need anything while we're away." Me avoiding Mom as much as possible. I don't want to ruin her special day, but I can't help feeling bitter.

Grace and I escape to the bathroom after dinner. "You wore the ugly dress?" She fusses with her hair in the mirror. She's worn it up and is completely transformed from earlier.

"It makes my mom happy."

"You're way too nice."

I shrug. I shouldn't need to explain that it's always been the two of us. Now, with the addition of Stanley, I'm not about to hurt our relationship by doing something she'll blatantly disapprove of.

"You look pretty," I tell her.

"Thanks."

Someone knocks on the door, but when we shuffle out, no one is there.

"Weird," Grace says.

I don't mention the haunted history of the restaurant, especially since it was a bride that tripped and fell down the stairs. The tragedy continued with the distraught groom committing suicide later that night. Some of the waiters say that when they clean at the end of the day, they see mysterious things. Mom said the whole story was silly, and I'm sure Grace would feel the same way.

"Want to get something to drink?" I ask. Grace nods. We stand at a table near the bar drinking sparkling cider. Blake comes over to join us. I realize he must not know many people and that this isn't necessarily a fun event for him, either.

"Let me take a picture," Grace says, motioning us closer together. I feel like she's taunting me since I said he was good-looking.

Blake puts his arm around my shoulder like he's known me for years. "That's a nice tie," Grace says. "The gray and pink looks good with El's dress. It's like you two belong together."

Definitely taunting me.

"Thanks," Blake says. "Ella helped pick it out."

My eyes widen. Grace can't realize that Blake was the beautiful boy from the mall. Even though it was an innocent mistake—how was I supposed to know I was gushing about my stepbrother?—I can predict how Grace will react. Shame flushes my cheeks as she snaps the photo.

I need to distract her. "Blake is new to Hoboken. A lot of movies were filmed here, right?"

That's the only cue Grace needs. She launches into a chronological history of Hoboken-related cinematography. Blake listens intently as I drift away to say hi to some of Mom's friends. Was his girlfriend disappointed not to be invited to the wedding? I can't help wondering if he's attracted to Grace. Not that I really care.

I spot Henry but steer clear of him. When I glance in his direction he's frowning at me. I'm relieved when Piper comes over, except that her dress is the same shade of pink as mine.

"Ooh, we match!" she says.

Great. I'm dressed like a nine-year-old.

"I can't wait for you to stay over," she says. "Grace is planning fun things. You'll include me, too, right?"

"It's up to your sister. You have to convince her."

"Mom says she's a mule," Piper says. "No one can convince her of anything."

I try not to laugh at her description of Grace's stubbornness.

When the waiters ask us to be seated for dessert, Blake and I are alone at our table as Mom and Stanley cut the wedding cake.

"She's interesting," Blake says about Grace, but it doesn't sound like a compliment.

"We've been friends for a long time."

"That's interesting, too. It seems like you would get on each other's nerves."

Don't all friends annoy each other sometimes? Although I realize it's been worse with Jana away. It's like we're a three-legged stool and Jana's absence leaves us unbalanced. I'm not sure how to respond to him, though, without being disloyal to Grace. Luckily, Mom and Stanley return and we all have cake. Mom makes chitchat in a breathless, happy way, only taking a few bites before they continue to socialize. Blake and I finish our dessert in silence.

"Would you like to dance?" he asks once we're done.

I follow him to the floor as "Fools Rush In" starts to play. Blake holds me at a respectful distance while we slow dance, but I still feel weird. Blake seems less like a stepbrother and more like an older friend from school. We have no real history together, nothing that makes him family. I wonder if anyone thinks it's odd that we're dancing.

"You're quiet," he says, making me realize how long I've been lost in my own thoughts.

"Sorry."

"I'm the one who's sorry. You obviously have a lot on your mind. I shouldn't have pushed you to learn about your dad. There's too much going on right now. You didn't need this."

I don't want to talk but it seems better to get it over with, like jumping right into the deep end of a cold pool. "You were right. I'm sorry I didn't believe you at first. The whole thing is kind of a surprise."

Blake shrugs. "It's understandable. Why should you believe me over your mom? Parents can suck when it comes to the truth. Not like us. We tell it like it is."

I'm not sure what to say to that. Are we bound by a vow of mutual honesty? Some type of sibling honor code? I don't think Grace and Piper are particularly truthful with each other. But there's a lot I don't know about being part of a larger family.

The song ends and Blake's hand lingers on my back. I feel the warmth through my ugly dress, but I push any unbrotherly thoughts of him out of my mind. Then Mom comes over and Blake wanders away.

"Is everything okay?" she asks. "You don't seem yourself tonight."

Of course she would notice, even between her hostess-bride duties. Mom knows me better than anyone. But I don't feel like I truly know her anymore. The force of the realization knocks me for a loop and I blink back tears.

"It's been an emotional day," I say, which is true, just not in the way that she expects.

"Yes, honey, it has. And you're still upset with me. It's about Oscar, isn't it?"

"I don't like being lied to." I make serious eye contact, somehow willing her to tell me the truth about everything.

"I'm sorry I wasn't honest sooner. I really am."

She looks so sincere and she doesn't hesitate at all. What about Dad, I want to ask her. What about the most significant lie?

"You need to always be truthful with me," I say. "I can deal with the facts, about Oscar or anything else."

"I promise."

I wait for more, for even a hint of a confession. It doesn't come.

# 10

# THE VISIT

I wake up late Sunday morning to find Blake making eggs in the kitchen.

"Dad texted that they boarded their flight. They didn't want to wake us this morning when they left," he says. "Want breakfast?"

Does he remember I'm a vegan? I stare at the eggs, wondering how to remind him politely.

He must see my expression. "Oh, the eggs are for me. Don't worry." He removes tinfoil from a plate on the counter. "For you, there's fake sausage and toast with weird pseudo-butter I found in the fridge." He pushes the food toward me. "Breakfast of champions! What are you doing today?"

"Working at the store."

"On a Sunday?"

"Mom picked the slowest time of year to go on her honeymoon, but there's still stuff to do, even if there aren't many customers."

"Maybe I'll tag along. You can start teaching me all the book stuff in case you ever want an afternoon off."

"Sure." It's nice that Blake's trying to be helpful and I do love that he made me breakfast.

After I eat, I feed Oscar. He sniffs it but only takes a few bites. I wonder if he misses Mom. I do, sort of. But given her dishonesty about Dad's death, it's a relief that she's gone. At least I have some space to think about what it all means and how I feel about it before I confront her.

Grace texts to see what I'm up to. When I tell her that Blake and I are heading to the bookstore, she asks to come, too. There's a new movie guide that she wants to order.

She shows up at our door a half hour later in a miniskirt and a green sleeveless shirt that shimmers. Whoa. I'm under-dressed in my shorts and T-shirt with a kitten wearing brainy glasses and a funky scarf. Hipster kitty.

"You look fancy," I say.

"Mom and I are going to lunch after."

When we arrive at the store, Henry collects his things as usual without talking to me. He gives me a nod on the way to the back.

"Henry doesn't like El," Grace explains to Blake.

"Grace!"

"It's the truth."

"It doesn't mean we have to tell people about it!"

I'm not sure why I care, but I do. Growing up without other kids, I usually have a good relationship with adults. But not Henry, for some reason. For all I know, he doesn't like anyone under the age of twenty. It still hurts my feelings.

"Let's order your book now," I say, hoping to distract her from any further Henry discussion.

Grace has never shown an interest in the bookstore operations before, but she listens politely as I show her and Blake how the special orders are processed. We find her latest must-see-before-you-die movie guide on the computer, place the order, and note Grace as the customer. "When the book arrives, we mark it into inventory and your name will pop up. We label it with a pricing sticker, then we let you know it's come in," I explain. "It should be here on Tuesday."

"Great. I should get going," she says.

"Have fun at lunch."

"Oh yeah, right. See you around seven?"

"Yes, thanks." Sleeping at Grace's is something to look forward to. I wonder what she'll say when I tell her about Mom's lies. It will be good to talk about it.

"Want to give me more training?" Blake asks. I show him how to work the register and he takes care of his first customer. Then he browses psychology books while I set up a back-to-school display.

My stomach growls at the end of our shift.

"Should we get takeout?" Blake asks. "Stanley and Andrea left us some spending money."

"My favorite vegetarian place is just past Third Street. Want to go? We can sit in the park and eat."

"Maybe I can meet you with a cheeseburger."

I laugh. "That would work, too."

Veggie Paradise is a small restaurant that mostly does a take-out business, but there are a few round tables by the front windows that always have pink carnations on them. Everyone calls the friendly owner Uncle Fred. I asked him once—he doesn't have any nieces or nephews in Hoboken. But "Uncle Fred" is even printed on his name tag.

"The usual?" he asks.

"Yes, please." They make a great veggie sandwich with hummus that I love.

"You are well?" he asks when he rings me up. "Still helping the cats?"

"Yes, thank you. Are you ready to adopt one?"

He laughs. "No, but you will be the first to know when I am. Have a delightful day," he says, handing me my bag.

I meet Blake in the park and we sit on a bench overlooking the Hudson. It's pleasant out, not too hot for a change. Mom calls while we're there, telling me about her jetlag and French food and Rodin sculptures. I mostly listen, trying not to hold a grudge about her lie. We keep the call short because of the expense, and I sit quietly after we hang up.

"You all right?" Blake asks.

"Just thinking about my dad. I wonder if he's mad I didn't know the truth all these years."

"I didn't know dead people had the capacity to be angry,"

he says. "Do you think you might be projecting your emotions a little?"

"Don't go all psychobabble on me," I say, even though he's right.

I hear a sad meow in the distance, a melancholy sound. "That's one unhappy cat."

"What cat?"

"You don't hear that crying?"

Blake shakes his head.

"That's strange." I don't want him to say I'm projecting my sadness onto a cat. "Maybe I'm just thinking about volunteering at the shelter tomorrow."

"That blue-haired guy from the bookstore is supposed to visit."

"Right." I don't want to get my hopes up. "If he even shows."

Mrs. Wallace makes us fresh popcorn to take to Grace's room for our movie night. Piper practically bounces into the kitchen like a kitten on catnip. "That smells yummy. I want to see the movie, too."

Grace sighs. "Mom, we're watching something too scary for Pippy."

"Don't call me that!"

"Okay, Pippy," Grace says.

"Mom, make her stop!"

It's going to be a long week. I don't know why antago-
nizing Piper brings Grace joy. Being an only child—well, for-
merly an only child—apparently has its benefits.

"Grace Elizabeth. Say you're sorry to your sister."

But Grace takes the bowl and leaves the room without
saying anything at all. I mouth "sorry" to Piper and follow
Grace up the stairs.

I need to tell her about Mom's lie, but she really wants to
watch the sequel to a poltergeist movie. We don't talk much
until it's over. I finally get a chance to explain how my dad
really died, how Stanley told Blake the truth about his death,
and how the psychiatric hospital sent the information. I talk
for maybe ten minutes, but it feels like hours have passed.

"I can't believe I didn't know the truth about Dad," I
finish.

"But . . . it's not like you had a relationship with him. I
mean, you never even met him."

It's as if Grace has smacked me. "I still *know* him. He's
my father." I pause and consciously stop myself from ranting.
Maybe it's my own fault she's never understood. Something
always kept me from telling her about his mysterious warning when I was young. But Grace could be harsh and I never
wanted to add to the list of things she made fun of at my
expense. "That's not the point. My mother lied to me. For
years."

"Can't you talk to her about it? It seems like if you confront her, she'll tell you the truth."

"I tried to give her a chance at the wedding. It was too awkward to bring it up directly. I don't feel like I can ask her on the phone during her honeymoon, either."

"You're right. It would be better face to face," Grace says.

We're silent for a few minutes. I imagine sitting in the kitchen across from Mom, calmly telling her about what I've learned. What would happen next?

"Besides," Grace says, bringing me back to the present, "maybe you shouldn't be too judgmental. Everyone lies sometime."

I stare at her. "Really? I'm not sure that's true. Or that it makes me feel any better."

"You never lie?" she asks.

"About what?" I can't figure out what she's hinting at, but I can tell by her crossed arms that she's annoyed about something.

"Remember the night before the wedding, when you rushed me off the phone?" Grace says. "You said your mom insisted that you get a good night's sleep, remember?"

*Uh-oh.*

"But at the wedding, Blake slipped up. He mentioned that you guys sat outside *drinking* together. Which I guess was more important than talking with me. At least you could have been honest about it."

"I—"

Grace keeps her arms tight over her chest. "Don't dig the hole any deeper."

"Sorry. You're right. I should have told you, but it's kind of awkward having a new family member. I felt like I had to form some type of friendship with him, that it was important to say yes. I didn't want to hurt your feelings."

"Whatever," she says.

"It's not really the same magnitude as Mom's lie."

Grace looks unappeased.

"I should've told you the truth. I can see why you'd be mad."

She sighs. "Okay, I guess I forgive you."

"That's good, since I'm sleeping here forever."

"How about a haunted marathon tonight? Are you ready for another movie? There's one about a sinister graveyard."

"I don't know. I'm home alone all week. Plus, I want to visit the cemetery tomorrow. It's not the best time for me to be freaked out about ghosts."

"You're not by yourself at home," Grace says. "Blake, that ultra-hot stepbrother of yours, is there, too."

I don't know how to react to that. She could have a crush on Blake, or she could be saying it to tease me.

"You know he has a girlfriend, right?" I say. She avoids my eyes as she hands me a blanket. "And I'm still not sure about ghost movies."

"If you don't want more ghosts, we'll watch serial killers instead."

"You're too kind, Grace."


In the morning, I stop at home to check on Oscar and drop off my overnight bag. Blake's door is closed, so I guess he's still sleeping. It feels important to keep my cemetery visit a secret from him. I'm not sure why. Maybe because he's already interfered with my memories of Dad, even if it isn't his fault that Mom lied. I slip out without waking him.

I could take the bus, but I walk quickly, eager to burn off the nervous energy buzzing through my body. I feel fidgety, agitated, like when several people enter the cattery at once, all looking to adopt a cat at the same time.

At the cemetery, I force myself not to hurry, making my way carefully through the tombstones. It's ridiculous, thinking that the cause of Dad's death changes anything. But somehow I feel different coming here today.

The ground is muddy, as if the grass has recently been watered. My walk leads me to Thomas Benton no matter how slowly I trudge. Thankfully, there are no more black flowers. Yet. I find a pebble and stand by Dad's tombstone, clasping it in my hand.

Dad has been my hero for so long. But now the story is

rewritten. I'm angry at Mom for lying to me, but I'm angry at Dad, too, for some reason. As if he could have told me the truth himself. Maybe it's more than that. What does an accidental overdose even mean? Was it his accident or someone else's?

I begin to wonder if the car crash and Oscar the Second are the only lies Mom has told me. What if Dad never saved Oscar the First from a storm drain? What if he was the grumpiest vet ever, wishing he'd been an accountant like Stanley instead? What if he loved lilies or weird black blossoms, and I've been leaving pebbles for years? Maybe I don't know Dad at all.

I lost him once. Now I'm losing him all over again.

As I leave my pebble, a piercing wail breaks my reverie. Shrubs and tombstones partially block my view, but I finally spot the source of the crying. Several rows away, a young girl shakes with loud, raw sobbing. The man she's with—her father?—puts a comforting hand on her shoulder. It does nothing to lessen the sound of her misery.

It weighs on me, this grief-filled air, buckling my knees. Before I know it I'm crying, too. It doesn't make sense to mourn Dad's death so intensely now, but the tears don't care about restraint and logic. They insist. Only weeping eases the heaviness. I kneel in the mud until I can breathe again.

Self-conscious about my outburst, I glance around as I rise to my feet. The father and daughter are gone, but other mourners remain. I recognize a squat gray-haired woman in the far corner: Norma. She doesn't seem to have noticed me. Part of me wants to rush away before she does.

But first I press my hand next to Dad's name, leaving a muddy handprint. "Happy birthday," I whisper.

I'm emotionally drained. The trek home feels longer than ever. Blake texts me while I walk—he's at the beach and will be home late. I'm relieved as I turn my key in the lock. It's nice to be home alone. I won't have to explain my post-cry puffy look.

"It's none of his business anyway," I say to Oscar, who's resting on the back of the couch. I take water from the fridge and press the cold bottle against my eyes for a minute.

My grimy hand leaves traces of brown on the plastic. I head to the bathroom to wash, using my elbow to flick the light switch.

I gasp. My dirty hand flies up to cover my mouth.

A muddy handprint mars the center of the mirror.

# 11

# SHELTER

I stare transfixed, trying to make sense of the handprint. I haven't touched the mirror. How could it be dirty?

Shivering, I retreat slowly from the bathroom. Then I creep through the apartment, checking to make sure I'm alone. No one else is here.

I don't get it. With Mom and Stanley away, Blake and I are the only ones using the bathroom. I didn't mess up the mirror. Maybe Blake did.

In the kitchen, I grab my phone. I want to call Mom, but that would be ridiculous. I dial Blake. It rings and rings. When I'm about to give up, he answers.

"Hey."

"Hi." I have no idea how to begin. "Um . . . are you coming home soon?"

"No. You got my text, right? I'm at the beach. Is everything all right? You sound strange. Like you have vegan indigestion."

How can I ask him about the random handprint over the

phone? I lose my nerve. He'll think I'm too weird. "Just checking in."

"Okay. See you later. Oh, and El? I lost my keys somewhere on the Jersey Shore. You'll need to buzz me in."

"Sure."

After we hang up, I open my water and take a drink. The only sound is my gulping. The building is oddly silent. There's no '80s music from Mr. Wilson's apartment down the hall, no random toilet flushing, no footsteps overhead. The quiet is disconcerting. The dead of summer must be a popular week for vacation.

I tiptoe to the bathroom, check the mirror. The handprint is still there. I think about wiping it, but I'd like to show Blake. It's a left hand, reminding me of my cemetery visit, but no one knows I went there.

Except Norma.

She could have seen me. As a building super, she does have a key. But why would she ever come in our apartment and do such an unusual thing?

I sit next to Oscar on the couch, leaning forward in case I need to escape quickly. I'm too fidgety to stay put. Even the normal fridge noises make me jump. After a quick change into my shelter T-shirt, I say good-bye to my sleepy cat.

I could be overthinking this whole thing. Of course, it seems eerie. But there's probably a logical explanation. Maybe Blake left a mess. That's what brothers do, right?

At the animal shelter, the beach party theme is in full

swing. Adorable Jersey City kittens have invaded from the damaged shelter, which is bad news for Petals. There's an especially cute gray one, Goedal, and even worse for Petals, a black fluff-ball named Mink. Her odds as an older black cat are looking worse.

I snuggle Petals in my arms. She's up to week number six at the shelter, which worries me. Hudson Animal Care and Control is a "full resources" facility, which means that when they run out of room, animals are euthanized. I witnessed an injection only once, when the shelter was short-staffed and needed someone to help with a cat named Freckles. He was old, but perfectly healthy, and I sobbed long after he drifted into his eternal sleep. There was something horrible about the unfairness of it all, about killing an animal before it physically needed to die. I've stuck to adoption and cat-socialization duties ever since then.

I circle the room, petting the other cats, adding water to the communal bowl, checking that the hand sanitizer is filled. I'm cleaning the litter boxes when the door opens.

A hunched, older woman comes in. Skyler told me that sometimes people find my over-eagerness unnerving, so I finish scooping poop and take the garbage out back while she looks around. When I return, she's still there. I straighten my HACC Volunteer T-shirt and try to assess her situation. It's a game I play, trying to guess people's pet history before they tell me. She has serious eyes behind her round glasses, but she moves self-assuredly like she's owned cats before.

"Let me know if I can help with anything," I say. "My name is Ella Benton."

"Hi, I'm Mrs. Brooks. My dear Grover passed away last spring, after a decade together."

"Grover, like from Sesame Street? We named my cat Oscar because he used to get into the trash."

She smiles. "I'm a retired history professor. He was named for the ex-president, Grover Cleveland."

Not the first Grover who comes to mind, but at least she's an experienced cat owner. She continues around the room, gently patting each cat. "I don't want a kitten," she says. "Something older."

"Great! Male or female?"

"It doesn't matter."

This is an adoption dream. The last couple who came in had been specific down to the eye color they wanted. But I don't want to be pushy about Petals.

"Well, we have Katniss." I stroke a Siamese-looking cat with blue eyes. "She's a stray, a bit independent. This is Carson." I pause in front of a tabby. "He's a bit of a rascal." I point to a white cat with black markings that look like a mustache. "That's Shakespeare."

"That face!" Mrs. Brooks says.

"Yes, he's very distinguished-looking." I show her Milo, Azula, Phoebe, Cinnamon, and the rest, saving Petals for last. I scoop her up. "They're all good cats, but this one, Petals, is one of my favorites. A family brought her in when they were moving and couldn't take her along. She's playful and very loving."

Mrs. Brooks strokes her black fur. "She has beautiful eyes." As if Petals is eager to make a good impression, she purrs loudly.

"Her information is here." I point to the wall, where we hang photos and large index cards with details about each cat. "She's spayed and up-to-date on all her shots."

"So, she's three?" she asks, peering at the card.

Uh-oh. The three is actually an eight. "Would you like to hold her?"

Mrs. Brooks gently takes her from me. "She is friendly."

I want her to adopt Petals, but I can't lie about her age. "Um, Mrs. Brooks? That's an eight on her card, not a three. But she's the nicest cat here. I wish I could bring her home myself."

"Eight is older than I want," she says. "Are these the only available cats?"

"Cattery Two is for cats that aren't ready to be adopted yet," I explain.

"Petals does seem loving," she says. "Let me think about it."

I nod, discreetly crossing my fingers for luck.

It's a busy afternoon and my shift goes by quickly. Mrs. Brooks lingers, holding one cat and then another. She doesn't say anything when she walks out, and I can only hope she's thinking over which cat to take home. I'm washing my hands when the cattery door opens and Gavin, the guy from the bookstore, walks in.

"Hey!" I inwardly cringe at my overly cheerful voice. "Are you ready to meet some cats?"

"Okay." He runs his hand through his hair as if he's nervous.

I introduce him to Petals, Cinnamon, who was named for her coloring, and the others. He scratches behind Cinnamon's ears, but doesn't seem anxious to hold any of them. What's up with this guy? When Milo rubs against his leg, he almost looks panicked. Does he even like cats? We spend an awkward fifteen minutes together before he clears his throat.

"Look, I'm sorry. I don't want to get too attached to any of the animals, because I haven't quite convinced my parents to let me adopt yet. I think I can persuade them, but I need a little more time."

His parents let him get a tattoo and dye his hair. It seems like a cat would be an easy sell. But if he's not ready to adopt, I'm tempted to ask why he's here.

"Of course," I say. "A parent would have to sign off on the adoption anyway if you're under eighteen. You live in Hoboken?"

"For the summer, with my cousin. Then it's back home to Parsippany for senior year."

That explains why I haven't seen him before.

"I'm sorry if I wasted your time," Gavin says.

"It's fine. I'm glad you met the animals. Petals is really my favorite. She's older, though, and some people are superstitious about black cats. It's been tough to find her a home."

"You seem enthusiastic. I'm sure you'll inspire someone to take her." He kneels to pet her, avoiding my eyes for a moment. "I should be getting to work soon. Is your shift almost over? I can walk with you as far as Hoboken Hardware and Locks."

I hesitate. He's not being entirely honest, I can tell. His attitude is off. I'm missing something—something below the surface. Then it dawns on me: Maybe he's not interested in visiting the cats at the shelter. Maybe he's actually visiting *me*.

"Okay. Let me finish up, and I'll meet you out front."

After rechecking the water bowl, I try to fix my hair. It's futile. As I sign out at the desk, Mrs. Brooks is filling out adoption paperwork. I discreetly take a peek. She's adopting Shakespeare. It's not Petals, but at least one of the older cats finally found a new home.

I head outside to meet Gavin. "Ready."

He has long legs but I keep pace with him.

"Do you like being in Hoboken for the summer?" I ask.

"It's easier to get a job here and I can walk wherever I need to go. I'm trying to save for a car. You work at the bookstore?"

"Yes, it's our family business. I'd like to help at a vet's office next summer if they'll hire me. For now, I volunteer at the shelter."

"You must really love animals."

"Definitely." As we walk, an unsettling thought wriggles in my mind. "How did you know I live in this direction?"

He shrugs. "Just a guess. I figured you live close to the bookstore. At least you get to work with family. My manager is a grouch. The hours are good, though, even if I spend my days making keys and stocking boxes of nails."

We near the ice cream shop. "I need to be at the hardware store soon," he says. "But I have time for ice cream. Should we stop here?"

"Sure." The invitation makes me nervously happy. We enter the shop and get in line.

"Waffle cone, raspberry sorbet," he orders. "What would you like?"

"I'll have the same thing. Raspberry sorbet is my favorite."

He smiles. "Maybe it's a sign."

I smile but can't think of a flirty comeback. "Maybe" is the best I can do.

We sit outside at a table with a striped umbrella and eat our matching cones. I steal glances at him when I can, wondering what a guy with blue-tinged hair going into senior year would find interesting about me. I suddenly feel self-conscious about licking my ice cream in front of someone I barely know. A cup with a spoon would have been better. When he's not looking, I stuff the rest of the cone in my mouth and chew.

Once we finish and start walking again, something is still bugging me, something that doesn't make sense. "I'm glad you got to meet the shelter cats," I say. "You bought those books so you'd be prepared. But would you adopt the cat in Hoboken, and then take it with you when you leave? Why not adopt when you move home?"

He smiles, sheepish. "I guess I haven't thought it all the way through."

His voice isn't convincing. I try to interpret his expression and nearly walk into a stroller in front of us. Before I collide with it, he takes my elbow and steers me clear. His hand is firm but gentle, and he doesn't let go right away.

"Maybe it seems surprising since I never had a cat," he says. "I read this book about an old cranky guy, not that I'm usually cranky, but his life is transformed by this cat he rescues. It's such a cool idea, to save a life and bond with a pet. I'm not used to being around animals, but I can't stop thinking about the ones that are stuck in shelters. And HACC is a kill shelter, right? So I wanted to save a cat from there."

"Oh!" I'm nearly speechless. We're reading the same book and he feels the same way about rescuing animals as I do. Wow.

We reach the hardware store. He shoves his hands in his pockets, looking uncertain. "Maybe we could get together again sometime?"

Even if Blake hadn't encouraged me to be open-minded, Gavin's shelter speech won me over. Of course, I'll owe Blake twenty dollars, and I'm tempted to say no, just to win the money. But not very tempted.

"That would be nice."

I float home because Gavin is sweet and interesting and wants to spend more time with me. Then I remember the weird handprint and the sunshine doesn't seem as cheerful. As I get closer to my street, tension bunches in my shoulders.

I'm relieved to see Blake sitting on the steps leading to our building. He has his head down, checking his phone with a beach towel slung over his shoulders.

"Why are you out here?" I ask.

He looks up, smiles. "Lost my keys, remember?"

"Oh, right. This is an odd question, but did you do any cleaning today?"

"Um, no. Was I supposed to?" he asks.

"I wondered if you did anything to get dirt all over your hands."

"Just sand." He stands and stretches. "Why?"

I lead the way inside, push the elevator call button. "Something weird happened this morning. I was out for a little while and when I came home . . . there's something I need you to see."

# 12

# THE DEAD

Blake and I stand in the bathroom, staring at the muddy handprint on the mirror.

"Tell me again," he says. "You came home . . ."

"Yes, I walked into the bathroom to wash my hands, and the handprint was there."

"You're sure you didn't touch the mirror?" Blake looks perplexed.

"Positive. I thought maybe you did it."

"I'm not left-handed." He leaves for a second, returns with a wet paper towel to clean up. "I'm sure there's a logical explanation. I wouldn't worry about this."

I can tell he thinks I somehow did it myself, accidentally touching the mirror without realizing it.

"It's creepy because . . ." I still don't want to tell him about the cemetery, about visiting Dad. "I mean, could someone have gotten in? Why would anyone do this?"

"From a psychology standpoint, it would be a bizarre thing to do. Who else has keys?"

I recite the list I'd compiled in my head: Mom, Stanley, Norma. "Oh wait—Grace has a key, too. We traded years ago. But don't tell Mom. We did it in case one of us got locked out. Our moms wouldn't let us keep one under the mat." I pause. "There was nothing on your key ring that would give our address, right? Could someone have found your keys and used them?"

"To sneak in and leave a handprint? I don't think so," Blake says. "Besides, they wouldn't know where we lived."

"Right, of course not."

I give up on solving the mystery for now and try to push thoughts of the cemetery visit out of my mind. Blake and I order pizza and watch TV until it arrives. Mine is cheese-less with vegetables.

"Was the beach crowded?" I assume he was with his girl-friend, even though he hasn't mentioned her specifically.

"Not bad. How was volunteering?"

"I owe you some money."

"For what?" he asks.

"The guy from the bookstore? He came into the shelter today and asked me out."

"Ha!" Blake says. "Not to say I told you so, but . . ."

"I know. You were right. Hey, he works at the hardware store. We can take my keys in and make a copy. But it could seem stalkerish if I show up there tonight."

"Let's wait until tomorrow," Blake says. "It'll give you an excuse to visit him."

After our dinner, Mom calls me. She's still not sleeping well, and I wonder if it could be her guilty conscience. Although, since she doesn't realize that I know about Dad, it's most likely the time adjustment. She tells me about a quaint French bookstore they visited.

"Everything's okay?" she asks.

"Yes. The building seems so quiet."

"The Heins are visiting their grandchildren," she says. "I think Dave down the hall left on a cruise. The Whiteleys mentioned they were going to Hawaii."

That would explain the lack of noise.

"Are you and Blake getting along?"

"It's been nice having him here." I go into my room and close the door. "It's Dad's birthday, you know."

"Right," she says, but I can tell from her voice that she forgot.

"I've been thinking about his death. A car accident—it was so sudden. It must have been hard on you. You never speak about it."

"It was horrible, El. But maybe we can talk about that another time?"

Obviously, she wouldn't open up about this now—long distance, during her honeymoon. I'm being a jerk.

"Of course," I say. "Sorry."

"I miss you."

"Miss you, too," I say. Especially with the handprint incident. But that doesn't lend itself to a phone conversation, either.

Later, I do get a chance to talk about it with Grace. During our sleepover, I tell her what happened, trying not to sound delusional.

"There must be a connection between the handprint at the cemetery and the one on my mirror," I say. "And my father's birthday is today, the eighth." Eighth month, eighth day. My lucky number. "It's also World Cat Day."

She ignores that last tidbit. "How could the handprint just appear? That doesn't make any sense."

"I know." I try to sound casual. "Hey, maybe we could have that séance tonight?"

"I was hoping you'd forget."

"His birthday is the perfect time."

"All right," she says. "Help me set it up."

While she goes to find matches and a candle, I clear off Grace's desk and move it to the center of her bedroom, with her chair on one side and a beanbag on the other. I pull down the shades, then turn out the lights. It's not really dark enough, so I cover her two windows with blankets. It will have to do.

I take out my favorite photo of Dad, which I'd carefully tucked into my overnight bag, and place it on the center of the wooden desk. The room is warm. I turn on the standing fan, sit in the chair, and wait.

Grace frowns when she returns. She seems unhappy about

my redecorating, but she only sighs. We've just lit the candle when Piper pops in to see what's going on. Grace sends her to bring in another seat.

"I'm babysitting," she says, as if I asked about Piper aloud. "I have strict instructions to include her."

Piper returns, dragging her desk chair, then places it right next to mine.

"I brought you some clothes and a few necklaces I don't wear anymore," I tell Piper. "I left the bag downstairs."

"Hooray!"

"Shh!" Grace says. "Let's get started. If we're going to have a séance, let's at least be serious like in the movies."

The fan rotates in my direction, then swoops away with a mesmerizing rhythm.

"Are you ready?" Grace asks. The flame flickers each time the fan blows.

I nod.

"Me first!" Piper says.

"Who do you want to communicate with?" Grace asks.

"Sparkles, of course!"

Her dead goldfish. I feel badly for Piper. I know how much I would miss Oscar if he died. He's a special part of the family. Piper had Sparkles for more than two years, which is like a hundred in fish life.

"Go ahead," I encourage her.

Grace presses her lips together in discontent.

"I miss you, Sparkles," Piper says to the ceiling.

"You have to ask a yes or no question," Grace explains. "One knock means no, two means yes."

I'm not sure why Grace thinks that's the best way to communicate, but I'm not about to argue. If I tell her everything I've researched about séances, it's sure to irritate her.

Piper breathes deeply, closes her eyes. "Do you miss me?" she whispers.

Silence.

"Do you miss me?" she asks again.

The only noise is the rhythmic hum of the fan.

"This is stupid!" Piper yells, bounding from the chair. "Goldfish can't knock, you big dummy!" She storms from the room.

"She's such a pain," Grace says.

"Shh. She might hear you. Don't hurt her feelings."

"You have no idea what having an annoying sister is like."

"True."

"Let's focus. Why don't you ask a question?" Grace takes my hands with the candle burning between us. She gives me a nod.

"Dad," I whisper. "Do you watch over me?"

I sound as foolish as Piper.

"Ask again."

"Do you watch over me, Dad?"

For a split second, the air shifts. It's like someone has entered the room. I hold my breath, but can't see anything. I'm afraid to be too hopeful, and honestly, I'm scared. The theory of ghosts and spirits is one thing. Experiencing a presence right next to me is another.

A bang comes from above us. Then a second. Two knocks. My heart leaps in my chest. Could it be?

The candle goes out. A stream of smoke swirls from the wick into the air.

My eyes adjust to the darkness, but I don't need any light to know goose bumps cover my arms.

A faint giggle drifts from the attic.

"Do you hear that?" I ask.

"The knocks?"

"No. Listen. It sounds like Piper laughing."

"PI-PER!" Grace yells her name in two angry syllables. "Get down here right now!" More giggles accompany the footsteps stomping down the stairs.

"I thought for a moment . . ." I frown. "The knocking was Piper. But the candle?"

Grace shrugs. "It must have been the fan."

"Why did it go out right then? The timing was surreal."

She flicks on the lights.

I blink in the sudden brightness. I don't try to explain the presence I felt to Grace. Even if I was afraid in that moment, it was wishful thinking that I could reach my father. I can't confuse desire with reality. Still, I spend a lot of time wondering about candles and handprints after Grace falls asleep.

If I'm going to entertain the thought that there might be a supernatural cause for the handprint, I have to first rule out any logical way it could have appeared. Not many people had access to our apartment. Not many people could have seen me leave a handprint on my father's tombstone.

In the morning, I wake with a plan to talk to Norma, the only possible cemetery witness.

Once I'm back at home, I carefully return Dad's photo to its hiding spot, then shoo Oscar from my laundry basket. I push my bras to the bottom, but I'm still grateful the elevator is empty so I don't have to feel awkward about my basket of dirty clothes. We have two coin-operated washers and two dryers for the whole building to share and they're all empty. Mom taught me to do wash when I was thirteen, and although I've always loved the smell of detergent and the satisfaction of putting clean clothes away, I've never been a fan of the back-and-forth to the basement.

After starting the wash, I survey the three lights overhead. The laundry basket is sturdy; flipped over, it's the perfect height to stand on for part one of my plan. I turn off the switch, then use my flashlight app so I can see to twist two of the bulbs. When I flip the lights back on, only one works. Perfect.

Norma's apartment is on the first floor. I take the stairs, hesitating only a moment before I knock.

"Who is it?" Her voice is old and weary even though she's about the same age as Mom.

"Ella Benton from the sixth floor."

She opens the door slowly. Her steel-wool hair is sticking

up, adding a good two inches to her short frame. I get the sense she doesn't spend a lot of time on her appearance.

"Hi. I wanted to talk to you about a problem in the basement."

"What's the matter?"

She doesn't invite me in, but I discreetly peer inside. Her home is impersonal, almost sterile. Still, I look for anything that might give me a sense of whether she'd break into our home and leave a handprint in the bathroom. Even as I glance over her shoulder I realize how ridiculous this is.

"Two of the lights are out in the laundry room."

"Two? Hmmph."

I realize my mistake: Two bulbs wouldn't burn out at the exact same time. I should have only turned off one. "It's, um, dark down there."

"Okay," she says. A dismissal.

I don't have a real plan and I'm not sure what details I expect to find, but it feels important to get inside and search more thoroughly. "Could I please use your bathroom?" Of course, I could go home, but I'm guessing that even gruff Norma won't deny me this.

"Come in," she says with a sigh.

I pause awkwardly in the kitchen. Her refrigerator lacks the photos that cover ours.

I stall. "If I were locked out while my mom is away, you have a key, right?"

Norma opens a gray metal cabinet on the kitchen wall.

It's filled with keys on hooks, all labeled. Ours hangs neatly among the others.

"Bathroom's down there." She motions her hand toward the hallway.

I feel her eyes on my back. Her apartment seems to be a mirrored version of ours. After closing the door, I'm tempted to check inside the cabinet and drawers, but it might make too much noise. What do I expect to find, anyway? A prescription bottle can't be the answer to my questions. I flush, then run water. Having come this far, I might as well explore. Leaving the bathroom, I quietly continue toward the nearest bedroom. I peek inside the open door and exhale slowly.

I'm face to face with a dead girl's shrine.

# 13

# DAUGHTER

From the doorway of the bedroom in Norma's apartment, I can see a huge photo of a girl about my age. She has long brown hair and brown eyes, like I do. Three candles are on one side of the ornate silver frame, a white teddy bear with a red bow on the other. Folded neatly in front is a red and white sleeveless jersey. The room smells like old flowers.

"What are you doing?" Norma shrieks.

I step back and drag my gaze away from the shrine. "Sorry, I went in the wrong direction. Your apartment is the opposite of ours. It's all backwards."

She slams the bedroom door. "Get out," she says. "I'll take care of the lightbulbs." Her eyes blaze with fury.

"Thank you." I leave Norma's and run down the stairs to the basement. The washer is still churning so I sit on the overturned basket to wait, tapping my foot nervously. I hope Norma doesn't show up in the next few minutes. I'd rather not talk to her again today.

The girl had to be Norma's daughter. That must be who she visits at Hoboken Hill Cemetery. But that didn't explain why she would possibly leave a handprint on my mirror. I'm not any closer to proving whether it was her or not.

Other than the chugging of the laundry in the washer, the basement is eerily quiet. I could go home, but the wash is almost done. I pass the time texting Grace, mostly complaining about not having our own laundry room. When the cycle finally ends, I toss everything into the dryer. A door slams somewhere in the building. The dim light creeps me out and I realize I should've pulled the lightbulb stunt *after* my laundry was finished. I hurry back to the apartment, relieved to see I'm not alone.

"Hey," Blake says. "Where've you been?"

"Doing laundry. Want to go to the hardware store soon?"

"Sounds good."

Gavin had given me his number, and before we leave, I text him that we're on our way. It seems less awkward than walking in unannounced. He texts back that he can't wait to see me.

I decide to change out of my T-shirt into a pale lavender blouse. I use mascara and lip gloss, but don't want to go overboard.

"You like this guy?" Blake asks.

"It's too soon to tell. Maybe."

"Did anything strange happen today?" he asks.

I tell him about Norma and my plan with the lightbulbs.

"I wanted the chance to talk to her, to scope out her apartment. Not that I expected to find anything concrete, but I hoped to learn more about her. She seems to be grieving. A muddy cleaning rag would have been a bonus—something she wiped her hands on after marking our mirror."

"Hmm. That was good thinking. You're more devious than I thought."

His compliment makes me happy. I don't like to think of myself as helpless, even in the face of bizarre events.

When we enter the hardware store, I introduce Blake to Gavin. I feel self-conscious in front of Blake, which he must realize because he quickly disappears down one of the aisles.

"Do you want me to copy the bookstore key for you, too?" I call after him.

"No, thanks," he says. "Too much responsibility."

Gavin takes his time with the keys, telling me his schedule for the day, asking about my bookstore and volunteer plans.

"Want to get together after your shift at the shelter tomorrow?" he asks. "We could have lunch."

"That would be nice." I smile.

Before I can embarrass myself with an overly gleeful reaction, Blake yells to me: "Come check this out."

I find him in aisle 3. He's holding a cat key holder with curved tails to hook the keys.

"Should we get it?" he asks.

"Yes! It's cute and practical, too. Mom will love it."

"Great." He pays for the keys and the key holder, I say

my good-byes to Gavin, then we head home. I don't know if Blake heard Gavin make plans with me, and I don't mention it. He doesn't need to know everything about my dating life.

In our lobby, he waits for the elevator. "I'll meet you up there," I say. "I need to get my stuff from the dryer."

I take the stairs down. Once the stairwell door closes behind me, the basement seems darker than ever, as if the electricity is off. The light on my phone helps guide me to the laundry room. I flick the switch. Nothing happens. Not even the one good light turns on.

Maybe Norma's in the middle of fixing the lightbulbs. She could have turned off the circuit breaker or something. But when I open the dryer, the drum light turns on as I dump the clothes into the basket. The electricity is working after all.

The light from the dryer illuminates the space and something catches my eye. I focus my phone on the wall to my left.

"No." I back up, banging into the open dryer door.

One word is scrawled in red capital letters across the wall: DAUGHTER. A bloody handprint drips in the space underneath.

I grab the basket. A cat T-shirt falls, but I don't stop. I need to escape, fast. The elevator takes forever. The doors slide open. I expect demons, monsters, ghouls. It's empty.

On our floor, I race to our apartment, fumble with my keys. My hands tremble too much to open the lock. "Blake!"

When he opens the door, I drop the basket to grab his arm. "Come with me."

"El, what's going on?"

I can't speak on the elevator ride to the basement.

"Seriously, are you okay? You're scaring me."

"I'll show you."

I turn my phone light on when we leave the elevator and pull him into the dark laundry room. I illuminate the wall but can't bear to look. "See?"

He's quiet. I figure he's as frightened as I am.

"See what?"

I turn my head and shine the light where the red scrawl was minutes before.

There's nothing.

"Why are we in the dark?" Blake asks, flipping the laundry room switch.

The lights come on. The sudden brightness makes me blink as I stare at the blank wall.

# 14

# LISTEN

I'm still shaking when we get back to the apartment.

"Are you sure you saw something?" Blake asks.

"Yes." I pet Oscar, trying to calm myself. "I'm positive. The word DAUGHTER and a handprint in red. Like blood. Don't you believe me?"

Blake sits next to me. I feel him inhale, exhale. "Of course. Let's think about this. Who could have done it?"

*My dead father. The day after his birthday.* But no. I search for a rational answer.

"The building super knew I was doing laundry. Like I told you, her teen daughter died. So that could be the daughter reference."

"Why would the super want to frighten you?"

"I don't know. Maybe she's unbalanced or something."

"Next time you do the wash I'm coming with you. And don't talk to her again."

"Okay." Is this what it's like to have a big brother—to have someone to protect you?

"What are you doing for the rest of today?" he asks.

"I think I'll stay here until it's time to leave for Grace's."

"All right. I'll walk you there later. Where do you keep the screwdriver? I'll hang the key holder."

I point him to the junk drawer. Relieved that he's around, I spend the afternoon transferring the wedding photos I took on to the computer so I can view them on a larger screen and weed out the bad ones. Once I've narrowed it down to the best fifty, I order prints and a small white photo album to put them in. It's a good distraction until it's time to head to Grace's.

Before I leave, Mom calls and keeps the conversation light and happy. I don't mention the laundry room incident, of course, or anything else about Dad. It will be better to talk to her in person. She'll be home in five more days. Somehow, we'll work through the whole lying thing. With all the latest weirdness, I'm feeling less angry at Mom at the moment.

Grace invites me for dinner before our sleepover. After I take care of Oscar, Blake walks me to her house. I feel safer with him by my side. Mrs. Wallace prepared make-your-own-tacos including refried beans and veggies so I could eat vegan and she could feed the rest of the family, too.

After dinner, Grace and I hang out in her room. Piper has apparently been banned, because she doesn't ask to join us, but I notice she's wearing the tiger's eye necklace that I left for her.

Grace flicks channels until she finds the original *Halloween*, which we've watched five times already. I tell her about Gavin visiting the shelter and our plans to see each other tomorrow.

"Whatever happened with the beautiful boy you met at the mall?" she asks. "No further sightings?"

"No. I guess it wasn't meant to be." I still can't bring myself to tell her that Beautiful Boy is Blake.

"That's too bad." Her tone is a little off. Maybe she's jealous over my possible late-summer romance with Gavin. The Tarot card reader did predict envy for her.

She won't be jealous over the latest handprint, that's for sure.

"There is something important I need to tell you," I say.

"What?" Grace sits up attentively.

The creepy *Halloween* music plays in the background and I shiver. "Would you mind turning that off?"

She uses the remote to mute the movie, but I can still see the villain, Michael Myers. I angle my body away from the screen and tell her about Norma and the laundry room.

"What's Norma's last name?"

"Morales."

Grace grabs her phone and types quickly.

"What are you doing?"

"Trying to learn more about Norma's daughter." After a few minutes of clicking, she pauses. "Wow, Ella."

Grace never calls me that unless it's serious.

"What?"

"Look at this photo. Her daughter looks just like you. You have the same brown hair, the same brown eyes."

I study Gina Morales on the screen. "Yeah, but so do half the girls in our school."

"You don't see the resemblance? Really? Because I bet Norma does."

I try to keep an open mind. "Maybe a little."

"It says that at age fifteen, Gina collapsed and died during a basketball game from an undiagnosed heart problem. She was buried at Hoboken Hill Cemetery six years ago."

I vaguely remember seeing Gina around our building, and then Mom telling me about her death. "Poor Norma." I imagine how upset Mom would be if anything happened to me.

"What if Norma is obsessed with you? You said you saw her at the cemetery, before all this creepiness started. She has keys to the whole building, right? Maybe your resemblance is a trigger for her to do bizarre things."

"Even if I resemble her daughter, that doesn't give her a motive. What does she gain by trying to creep me out? And if she left the message in the laundry room, why erase it so quickly?"

"To avoid getting caught? Who knows," Grace says. "Maybe grief changes how someone thinks."

Out of the corner of my eye, I see the killer carrying a body across the screen. "Can we *please* turn that off?" I sound angrier than I intend.

Grace finally clicks the remote. "Norma could be mentally ill."

I pause at the words "mentally ill." Didn't she listen to what I told her about my dad? "Let's forget about it for tonight."

"Maybe we should go to bed," Grace says. "I'm tired."

It's too hot to climb inside the sleeping bag, so I settle on top of it with a blanket next to Grace's bed. We turn out the lights, but when her phone pings with a text, Grace doesn't seem tired at all. The light from the screen illuminates the room as she taps away, making it impossible for me to fall asleep. She smiles as she types, but when she finally turns off her phone, she doesn't bother to tell me who the text is from.

I wake up several times during the night from bad dreams I can't quite remember. In the morning, Grace seems distant toward me and we barely speak. As I gather my clothes, I realize I'd rather sleep in my own room for a change. I won't come back tonight.

At home, the apartment is eerily quiet. I cautiously peek in the bathroom, but it remains handprint-free. I walk through Mom's bedroom and then enter Blake's room. I don't know where he's spending the afternoon. His neatly made bed doesn't look slept in. An NYU course catalog rests on his nightstand, along with a guide to Spanish-speaking coun-tries, and a memoir about a sociopathic father. Psychology research, no doubt. Tucked behind the books is a framed picture of a young Blake, a barely recognizable Stanley, and a pretty woman who must be his mom, Veronique. His open suitcase rests on the floor at the foot of the bed, filled with neatly folded clothes. I guess barely unpacking would make going to school that much easier. He must be shipping the rest of his stuff directly to the dorm from his mom's house.

I realize that I'm moving stealthily, as if I might disturb someone. Or something. I leave Blake's room and sit on the edge of the couch. I've never felt so shaky. It's like my childhood home has been transformed into a haunted house. Every shadow needs a second glance, every noise a closer listen. What am I scared of?

The answer comes to me like a horror movie whisper: I'm afraid of ghosts. My dead father's spirit reaching out from the grave, trying to come to emotional closure as his beloved family moves on.

No. I'm losing it. Maybe the person that needs emotional closure is me. My phone rings, and the sound makes me jump. It's Gavin.

"Hey," he says.

"Hi."

"I just wanted you to know I was thinking of you. We're still good for a late lunch, right?"

"Yes. I'm on my way to the shelter in a few minutes. See you after my shift."

On the way to volunteer, I can't help thinking about Gina

Morales, about how sad and lonely her mother must be. Norma doesn't even have a pet to keep her company. I wonder if she is allergic to cats. My brain spins with the adoption-matchmaking possibilities. If Norma adopted Petals, I could visit her! But I need to rein in the fantasy. She never seemed remotely warm toward Oscar.

Once my shift starts, I spend my usual cuddle time with Petals until a couple comes in. They want a younger cat, but not a kitten, so I encourage them to take Cinnamon. This helps pass the time, but I can't help checking the wall clock every few minutes.

At exactly two o'clock, Gavin breezes through the door wearing a backpack.

"Hi," he says. "How's adoption-land today?"

Petals jumps from my arms to greet him. Then Carson comes over, followed by Azula, Katniss, and Goedal. Soon all the cats surround him.

"Have you become the cat whisperer?" I ask, laughing.

"It must be the backpack. I brought our lunch. Plus some cat treats so they'd like me."

"Uh-oh. You can't feed them outside treats. It's against shelter rules."

"Oops," he says. Azula starts to meow loudly.

"We have to leave before you start a riot. You go first, and I'll make sure none of them sneak out behind you."

I have to gently move Carson away from the door before I can follow Gavin to the lobby.

"Are you hungry?" he asks.

"Starved."

"Good. I know the perfect place for a picnic."

We pass Henry on the way, but he's on the other side of the street and doesn't see me. I don't go out of my way to say hello.

Soon we arrive at the castle entrance of the Stevens Institute of Technology. Trees create a canopy over the main path and the shade feels delicious in the midst of the summer heat.

I'm too nervous to be chatty. I haven't told Gavin that I'm a vegan, and I don't want to make him feel bad about whatever lunch he brought. I'm hoping for PB&J or something that I can deconstruct without hurting his feelings.

We continue uphill. It's so hot that the air-conditioning creates condensation on the windows of the buildings we pass. Summer-school students are hunched over their computers inside.

"Castle Point is the highest part of Hoboken," Gavin says. "That's one of the college's claims to fame. The land was purchased by the Stevens family in 1784. There's a lot of interesting history here, including stories about a campus ghost."

"Really?" I shiver despite myself.

"His name is Jan of Rotterham. According to the online student handbook, his favorite time to haunt the campus is on windy March nights."

"How do you know all this? Are you applying to go to school here?"

"I'm kind of a Hoboken history buff."

"Do you know Sybil's Cave on Sinatra Drive? The story about Mary Rogers? Her murdered body was found in the Hudson River in the 1800s, near the entrance to the cavern."

Gavin nods. "Edgar Allan Poe altered her name and based 'The Mystery of Marie Rogêt' on the case. He changed the setting to Paris, though. I guess Hoboken wasn't exotic enough."

I'm amazed that he knows so much about this particular story, too. "They never did figure out who killed her."

We reach Castle Point. I haven't been here in ages and the view is stunning today—we can see from the Verrazano Bridge on the right to beyond the Empire State Building on the left. There are a few picnic tables in the area, but Gavin walks over to a large oak tree. He unzips his backpack and spreads a striped sheet on the ground, then takes out a bag from Veggie Paradise.

"I hope you don't mind some vegan food," he says, motioning for me to sit beside him.

I'm so happy that I nearly bounce onto the sheet. "This is perfect. I've been a vegan for a year now. How about you?"

"Not quite that long," he says.

"Isn't Uncle Fred the best?"

"Who?"

"You must know Uncle Fred if you go to Veggie Paradise," I say. "He's super friendly."

"Oh, yeah, that guy." Gavin divvies up the hummus and veggie sandwiches on paper plates and we eat. Each ripple of the Hudson River shimmers in the sun. It looks almost magical.

I lean back on my elbows, taking in the beauty of it all. Gavin lies next to me and our breathing becomes synchronized. His tattooed arm is nearly touching mine. I'm tempted to trace the intricate black design with my index finger. "Why did you choose that pattern for your tattoo?"

"It's a Celtic rose," he explains. "My parents are first-generation Irish."

A rose. Yet another black flower to appear this month. I want to ask him more, but he leans toward me and his lips brush my cheek. I hold my breath, unwilling to move, to do anything that might ruin this moment.

A cat cries in the distance. I try to ignore it, because Gavin entwines his fingers in mine. It's like waking from a dream that I don't want to end.

The cat cries again, a plaintive sound, like when Oscar got sick a few years ago and the vet's assistant had to pry him out of my arms so he could be examined. Gently, I pull away from Gavin and tilt my head to one side. The cat sounds a lot like Oscar.

I stand, focusing on the noises around us. "Do you hear that?"

Gavin scrunches his brow, looking guilty. No, not guilty. Miserable. I think he was about to kiss me again before the cat cried.

"Hear what?" he asks.

I listen with my whole being. An unhappy meow breaks the silence.

"That! The cat! It sounds close by."

Gavin doesn't answer.

"You don't hear it?" The sound repeats, and I can swear it's Oscar. I take a few steps toward the building on our left and approach the patio area. Could a sick cat have wandered onto it? Or could Oscar have gotten loose and followed us here?

Gavin jumps up. "Wait—"

"Oscar?" The answering cry seems louder than before.

Gavin glances around, looking desperate and worried.

"I have to find him."

He takes my hand, squeezes. "El."

Something in the way he says my name makes me pause.

"El, I don't . . . I don't hear anything."

"Listen. You don't hear that sad meowing?"

"No."

A helicopter flies overhead. After it passes, there's quiet except for the leaves shimmying overhead.

"You never heard it?" I whisper.

Gavin doesn't answer. He turns his face away, as if embarrassed for me.

# 15

# COMPLAINT

Gavin walks me home from our picnic. He stares at the ground when we say good-bye and doesn't make plans to see me again.

I try to think of a rational explanation for hearing a cat cry when Gavin didn't. Am I subconsciously worried about Oscar? Does Gavin have bad hearing? Did I really imagine it? I can't come up with a satisfying answer. My brain buzzes as if I've had too much caffeine. I need to keep moving.

Once Gavin is out of sight, I hurry away from my apartment building and immerse myself in the crowd across the street at the Hoboken Terminal. The cat incident makes me unsettled. What I really need to do is make sure Oscar is all right. But I'm afraid to check.

On impulse, I buy a ferry ticket and board. Not many people are heading toward Manhattan, so the ride is peaceful and soothing. My heartbeat finally slows. From the boat, I strain to guess which building on the Hoboken shoreline might be part of the Stevens campus.

I head to the upper deck to get a better view. On an empty row of chairs in front of me, someone left a basketball behind. The ball makes me think of Gina Morales, her sudden death, and the DAUGHTER message.

I shiver as I pick up the ball, turn it over in my hands. I'm tired of odd coincidences. Could it be a sign from one daughter to another? I almost expect to see a big "GM" written on it, but there's no way to identify its owner.

Just then, a young boy jogs up the steps. "You found my ball! Thank you."

I hand it to him and he leaves, smiling.

I seriously need to get a grip.

I don't disembark in Manhattan and instead stay on the ferry for the return trip. When it docks again in Hoboken, I make my way home. Oscar sleeps peacefully on top of my bookcase while Blake watches TV in the family room. Relieved that everything is normal, I sit with Blake on the couch and catch the end of *Dumbest Crooks Ever*. It's a big fat dose of karma when the stupid people get caught.

"How was your date with Gavin?" Blake asks when the show ends.

"He's almost too good to be true. A cute vegan potential cat-adopter." I don't mention the ghost stories and the cat only I could hear.

"And you told me he wasn't your type," he says. "Maybe you should invite him over for dinner one night."

"Maybe." I wonder if Blake's girlfriend would come, too. He hasn't said much about her lately.

"Oh, Norma was in the elevator with me before. She got out on our floor."

"Really? Well, she is the super. There could be a legit reason."

"Still, it made me a little uneasy. What time are you going to Grace's? I can walk you there again."

"Thanks, but I decided to stay home tonight." I don't explain why. "Besides, if Norma saw you, then she knows I'm not alone, right?"

"Look. I have to confess something. I haven't actually been sleeping here. I've been pet-sitting for my friend's dog and I promised to take care of her for two more nights. Zoey hates to be alone for long. Are you sure you don't want to go to Grace's?"

"Could you bring the dog here instead?"

"What about Oscar?" he asks.

"You're right, that wouldn't work." But I've already made up my mind about Grace. "I'll be fine here alone." I hope. I just need to make sure that my imagination doesn't get the best of me.

After we eat some dinners Mom froze for us, Blake decides to check on the dog, then come back to our apartment to keep me company before he leaves for the night. I'm a little antsy while he's gone but nothing out of the ordinary happens. I text Grace to tell her I'm sleeping at home. She doesn't text back.

Blake returns with two tall white cups and straws. "Milk shakes," he says. "Yours is without the milk, of course. I bought you some smoothie thing instead."

"Thanks." I take a sip, pleased that he thought of me. "This is delicious. Berry is my favorite."

"Yeah, I noticed the inventory of pink vegan sorbet things in the freezer." He puts out his hand, palm up. "You owe me some money."

"Sure. How much was it?"

"Not for the milk shake. For the bet about your date."

"You're right, you won." I go to my room to get the cash. Oscar hasn't moved from his spot, and I'm relieved that he's not crying like the mystery cat I thought I heard.

I take two fives and a ten out of my wallet and hand them over to Blake. We watch some more mindless TV before he glances at his phone. "I should get back to Zoey. I'll keep my phone on if you need me." He grabs his keys from the new cat holder he hung near the door.

I don't really want to be alone here tonight, but then again, I don't want Blake to think he needs to babysit me. I try to sound casual. "See you tomorrow."

After locking the door, I flip through the TV channels but nothing holds my interest. I decide to text Jana. Her grandma strongly discourages electronics, but I figure Jana can sneak a few texts to me. Sure enough, she answers, telling me about the beach and the shells she found. I tell her about Gavin, which feels like the safest thing to talk about in my bizarre, mixed-up life.

"That's funny," she texts. "You and Grace both—"

She doesn't finish the sentence. I answer with a bunch of question marks, but her grandma must've become suspicious. Jana doesn't respond. I'm about to call Grace and ask what Jana meant when someone bangs on the door.

I freeze. A sudden knock at the door is not a frequent sound, because you have to buzz people into the building. You always know when someone's coming. For someone to knock unexpectedly means that they were already buzzed in or that they live here.

I look through the peephole. It's Norma.

Just the sight of her gives me chills. She's the building super, so I can't ignore her. I call out instead of opening the door. "Hi, Norma. What's going on?" The glass circle distorts her shape, making her look even scarier.

"Mr. Hein would appreciate it if you'd turn the music down."

I blink. "What?"

"The music that you were blasting. I could barely hear him when he called. He said it came from the apartment right below him. That would be you."

"I haven't been listening to any music."

"That's what you say. I heard it loud and clear through the phone."

"All right." I give up on proving my innocence. "There's no music now. He should be happy."

She stomps off, making a lot of noise for a small person. I move away from the door, and even though I know it's already locked, I double check just in case.

I change for bed but can't sleep, even with Oscar snuggled against me. I'd been texting Jana, not listening to music. What was Mr. Hein complaining about?

OMG. I sit up so fast that it jostles Oscar. Annoyed, he moves to the top of the bookcase.

Mr. Hein couldn't have called Norma. He's away on vacation! Mom mentioned it when I told her the building seemed quiet. He's traveling someplace with his wife and grandchildren. I'm sure of it. So he definitely didn't call and complain about anything.

Norma must have made up the whole thing. But why would she lie? She could be checking on me, making an excuse to see if I'm home.

I keep my eyes open as long as I can. It wasn't a good idea to stay here alone. Despite my nervousness, though, I'm exhausted. I'm half asleep when Gavin texts me. Could we see each other tomorrow night? I say yes, glad that he doesn't care about the cat-crying weirdness after all. We text until the adrenaline from Norma's visit passes. I don't remember saying good night to Gavin before my eyes close.

In the morning, I wake slowly. I blink a few times, check the clock—I slept a solid eleven hours. I lean over and rub Oscar, who must have come down from the bookcase to resume his usual spot in bed. He purrs and the soothing sound puts me back to sleep.

An hour later, I wake up and stretch my arms overhead. It takes me a minute to notice them.

Handprints.

Bloody handprints mark my bedroom wall.

# 16

# BLOOD RED

Eight bloody handprints mar the wall by my window. I pull the covers to my chin and shrink back against the headboard as if that will somehow help. It doesn't. I close my eyes, willing everything to be normal. Maybe the images will disappear like they did in the laundry room. Maybe I'm imagining them like the cat crying. Sitting with my eyes closed makes me even more nervous. What if something is in the apartment and it sneaks up on me while I'm hiding in bed?

I make myself open my eyes and look. The red prints are still there.

I fumble for my phone on the nightstand. Blake doesn't answer when I call, but I reach Grace.

"Can you come over? Now? It's important."

"What's the matter?"

"I can't explain. I'll show you when you get here."

"Okay," she says. "See you soon."

Knowing help is on the way, I breathe deeply and creep

out of bed to inspect my wall from a distance. The prints start by the bottom windowsill and face upward, four left-handed prints on each side, symmetrically climbing the wall. Long, distorted fingers streak the topmost one, making it creepier than the others.

I back out of my bedroom. A quick scan of the rest of the apartment tells me I'm alone and the door is still locked.

How did the handprints get there? Even with a key, Norma would have to be quite the ninja to enter my room and do this without waking me. I sink into the couch and try to remember all the weirdness that's happened so far. Dad's photo fell out of its album. The muddy handprint in the bathroom mimicked my cemetery visit. When I was out with Blake, the second print appeared in blood with the word DAUGHTER in the basement. The mysterious cat cried. Then this happened while I slept.

Everything connects to my visit to the cemetery and to cats. To Dad.

And to me.

I'm Dad's daughter—the daughter who visited the cemetery, the one who left the first handprint. I always wanted him to watch over me. But I definitely didn't want to interact with the spirit world like this.

My phone rings a while later. It's Grace's home phone, which she rarely uses.

"Grace?"

"No, it's me. Piper."

"Hi, Piper. Is everything okay?"

"Yes. I mean, no. I'm fine. I just have to show you something. Are you coming over today?"

"I'm not sure. Grace is on her way here now."

"Never mind." Her voice gets pouty.

"What do you want to show me?"

"I was in Grace's room. Just for a minute. I was *not* snooping. It's on her bulletin board. You know, where she saves special things? The badge."

"What badge?" The buzzer sounds. I hit the unlock button. "She's here, Piper. I need to go."

"I just wanted you to know about the beach badge. Thanks for the clothes and stuff."

I'm confused about why Piper feels a beach badge is important. We hang up right before Grace knocks on the door.

"What's the crisis?" She's holding a cup of coffee from the deli on the corner. It smells like hazelnut.

"You stopped for coffee?"

"I couldn't think of many emergencies that trump caffeine."

"I guess. But you have to see this."

I hold my breath as I lead her to my room, wondering if the prints would disappear again. Which would be better: hallucinations or the actual physical evidence that someone— or something—was in my bedroom last night? Both options are a big problem.

The handprints are still there. I exhale. It's a picture-worth-a-thousand-words moment.

"You see those, right?" I point, just in case.

Grace nods.

Even though the situation is scary, I feel calmer already. It isn't my imagination. Grace is my witness.

"They were there when I woke up. I never heard anyone come into the apartment."

"Where's Blake?"

"He had to dog-sit for a friend and he slept there," I say. "He's not home yet."

"Oh." She pauses. "And nothing strange happened last night?"

"Norma stopped by. I didn't open the door, and I don't know how a person could sneak in without waking me. I know you don't believe in the supernatural anymore, so this is going to sound crazy." I need her opinion, because she's skeptical and sane. "Do you think it's a ghost?" I whisper.

Grace frowns. "You've lived here forever. Why would a ghost haunt you now? Do you think it's Gina Morales?"

"The prints are left-handed. My dad was a lefty, like me. This started before the wedding, when the photograph of Dad showed up on the floor and I couldn't figure out how it got there."

"You never mentioned the photo."

"That's when I asked you about your hiding spot," I explain. "Since I went to the cemetery on his birthday, things have been worse. The number of handprints went from one to eight, and they changed from mud to blood."

Grace studies the prints. "It doesn't look exactly like blood. Can I touch them?"

"Of course."

Grace runs her index finger through the lowest print on the right. Then she moves her face near the wall and sniffs the redness.

"It's not blood," she announces. "It's paint, like the kids' stuff we use at the daycare."

"Paint? A ghost who uses paint?" I ask, bewildered.

"No, a ghost wouldn't. A person would." She sighs. "Could someone have leaned in through the window? You could reach the wall from the fire escape."

I approach the window, slowly, as if the prints might materialize into actual hands and grab me. "Locked."

She places her left hand over one of the prints and it's a pretty close match. Stepping back, she taps her lip with her finger.

"Weird," she says. "You didn't hear anything last night?"

"Nothing at all. Can you take photos while I measure them? I feel like we need evidence, some way to look at this analytically." She puts down her coffee and grabs my phone from the nightstand while I dig for the white ASPCA ruler in my desk. I hold the ruler next to the handprints as she photographs them.

"Straighten it out," she says, clicking away.

"Thank you for helping."

She nods, but when I reach to take my phone back, she freezes.

"What?" I ask.

I follow her gaze to my outstretched hand. Traces of red streak my palm.

# 17

# DECEPTION

Grace looks at my stained left hand, then at the prints on the wall. Her eyes squint in fury, her mouth is pressed tight.

"What's going on, Ella?"

I shake my head back and forth, at a loss for words. "I don't know." It feels like I'm speaking with a mouthful of cotton.

"Is this a joke? Are you that desperate for attention?"

"What do you mean?" I waver between anger and confusion. "I don't know why my hand is red. I didn't make those handprints. You have to believe me. Do you think I'm sleepwalking or . . . I don't know? There has to be an explanation."

"You could be lying, like when you met Blake outside that night." Grace looks at me skeptically. "Are you sure there isn't anything else you want to tell me?"

My eyes dart around the room. Her tone says that yes, there is something else I want to tell her. But my thoughts come in slow motion, like when I take allergy medicine that makes me groggy. Something about Piper's mention of the beach is bothering me. . . .

"What about Blake's tie?" Grace asks.

I think about seeing him at the mall, not knowing he was my stepbrother. I stall. "Um—"

"*He* was the beautiful boy. You never admitted that, either, even when I asked you about him later."

"Grace, I was mortified. That's the truth. Once I found out who he was, I felt so stupid about my reaction, my going on about him. You would think the whole thing was gross, even if I didn't know who he was. But my embarrassment—that has nothing to do with the creepy handprints on my wall."

"Blake warned me you'd react badly to our relationship, but I didn't expect *this*."

"What relationship? You and Blake are together?" I stare at her, my oldest friend. Grace, who defended me, with her hands on her hips, when a teacher mistakenly thought I cheated on a test. Grace, who helps decorate the animal shelter Christmas tree each year. Grace, who is now romantically involved with my stepbrother, having private conversations about me. "I didn't realize about you and Blake. Talk about people keeping secrets! Why didn't you tell me?"

"Blake asked me not to yet," Grace says matter-of-factly. "I knew you'd figure it out on your own. But I didn't expect anything as elaborate as this to make you the center of his attention."

My head spins with the repercussions. How long has this been going on? Why would she listen to him instead of being loyal to me? I can only fight one battle at a time, and right now the bizarre handprints take precedence.

"Look." I'm determined to convince her. "Let's forget about you and Blake for a moment. I don't know how the handprints got here. I couldn't have done it. That doesn't make any sense. The ones in the bathroom and the basement were there when I walked in."

She shakes her head sadly, as if she's incredibly disappointed in me. "No one saw the one in the basement but you."

"I'm not making this up!"

"I have to go," she says.

The door slams behind her. I rest on the edge of my bed for a moment. What just happened? In all fairness, I hadn't been entirely honest with her lately, but her and Blake? To top it all off, she actually thinks I would stage this scene because I was angry at her for dating my stepbrother.

I can't stand looking at the handprints anymore. I throw out Grace's coffee cup, then I wipe my walls with spray cleaner and paper towels. I do it quickly, as if it's another regular mess, like cleaning up Oscar's hairballs. Once I'm finished, I wash my hands, staring as the red splatters on the sink before the water swirls it away.

I don't know what to do next. There's a text from Mom, checking in. I pick up my phone to call her, put it back down.

How can I explain any of this? I can't worry her during her last days of honeymoon bliss. Three more days and she'll be back. Things will have to return to normal then.

For now, staying in the apartment alone makes me skittish. I need to leave. Getting dressed quickly, I think through all that I know. There were handprints on my wall and paint on my hands. Yet, I certainly didn't mark my own walls. Do we even own red paint? I rummage through the drawer where Mom kept craft supplies when I was younger. Kitchen utensils have migrated there now, so serving spoons mix with magic markers. No paint.

I would definitely hear someone enter my room. Wouldn't I? If I didn't make the prints and nobody entered my room, then that leaves only one explanation: the paranormal. I've never discounted the supernatural the way Grace does, the way Mom does. It seems possible.

Mom's remarriage could've upset Dad. Maybe he's decided to connect with us, with me, like when he warned me to wait right before the car crashed onto the sidewalk. For all I know, he tried again since that time by moving his photo or other things. There have always been instances of misplaced items. I would find my sweatshirt in the kitchen when I could swear I put in my bedroom. Stupid stuff like that. Maybe Dad has been reaching out to us all along. Now, he's just stepped it up a bit.

Could I have touched the paint during the night, been drawn to Dad's presence? I don't know how ghosts work with objects in our world. I need to visit the cemetery again soon, to make peace with him. That seems to be the only way to make this stop.

I put on my sandals, wondering how long it will take to make peace with Grace. I'm still shocked about her and Blake and the fact that neither one of them told me.

The beach badge. Now what Piper said makes sense. The day Blake lost his keys on the Jersey Shore, he must have been with Grace. All the beaches charge a fee and the pin-on badge shows it was paid. Was that their first date? What about the girlfriend he told me he had—the one I never met?

I decide to eat my breakfast out, in the safety of a public place. First, I fill Oscar's food bowl, but he doesn't come. With all the commotion over the handprints, he's been neglected today. I find him under my bed with his eyes closed.

"Oscar?"

He won't wake up. Even when I put a treat to his nose, he stays asleep.

"Oscar!"

I gently slide him from under the bed. He's breathing but unconscious. Usually he would howl in protest when I place him into his carrier, but there's only a horrible silence as I move him now. I rush from the apartment into the elevator and burst outside, hail a cab, and head to the vet's office. My hands shake, but I have to hold it together, have to think clearly for Oscar's sake.

I manage to dial the vet from the car to tell him I'm coming.

Once I arrive, there's a flurry of activity and no time to even kiss my Oscar good-bye as they lift his limp body out of the carrier and rush away. Trying to stay calm, I answer all of the doctor's questions about loss of appetite and lethargy. The vet seems worried, too, but he reassures me they'll take good care of him. I leave my cell and home numbers so they can contact me if there's any change in his condition.

I sob on the lonely walk home, not bothering to wipe the tears away.

# 18

# HAUNTED

I need to stay busy to keep from obsessing over Oscar. Thankfully, my bookstore shift is on the schedule today. I don't hear from Grace or Blake, which is just as well. Maybe they're spending time together. It's none of my business, I try to tell myself. It doesn't make me feel any better.

At the bookstore, I skim the cat medical books we carry, but the disease descriptions leave me more anxious. Henry makes himself scarce again. The only time we talk is when I notice that a container gardening book he wanted has come in. I start to process the other special orders, but it's hard to concentrate while I repeatedly check for messages from the vet. I scan the displays for misplaced books and neaten the shelves instead.

After work, the apartment feels deserted without Oscar. The vet finally calls: They've stabilized him but want to run tests to figure out the cause of his illness. He's improved, which is good news, but the vet is cautious about promising anything about his recovery. I breathe deeply for what feels like the first time all day. I explain about my mother being away, and he says not to worry about the bill, that they'll mail it to Mom. Well, Mom and Stanley now.

I'm literally staring at the wall when Gavin texts, saying he'll see me in an hour. Our date! I've completely forgotten. I'm tempted to cancel, but honestly, it would be nice to have a distraction. It's lonely at home without my favorite fur ball.

When I buzz Gavin up and open the door, he's wearing black pants, a white dress shirt, and a bow tie the color of his hair. My jean shorts are obviously all wrong for wherever we're headed.

"Are we going someplace, um, fancy?" I stammer. "I can change."

He laughs. "You're fine. This is my uniform. I'm taking you out with me on my second job. I work as a guide for Haunted Hoboken, but no one signed up for tonight."

"Haunted Hoboken?"

"You get your own private tour."

I'm about to back out, to say the whole thing is a bad idea. Creepy things like blood-red handprints, black flowers, and the scrawled "daughter" flash through my mind. But Gavin seems sincere, as if he's put a lot of thought into this, and he looks so handsome dressed up.

"I would feel better if I changed. Give me two minutes," I say.

When I come out in the yellow dress Blake bought me, Gavin's eyes get wide. "You look beautiful."

"Thank you. So, why didn't you mention this other job?"

He shrugs. "It never came up, I guess. It's a new branch of the New York version and it pays well enough."

Once we get to the street, he announces with a flourish and a bow, "Welcome to the official Haunted Hoboken tour. I'll be your spiritual guide. The first stop on this grand adventure will be The Brass Rail."

My smile is strained. Of course, I know the restaurant's ghost story. With all that's happened lately, I'm not entirely in the mood for haunted anything.

Gavin chatters most of the way to the restaurant, mainly about Hoboken's history. "That Hotel Victor sign?" He points. "It's been there since 1935. At one point, City Hall used to be a public marketplace." We don't pass the library, but he lets me know it was the third one in all of New Jersey.

"It must've been hard to memorize all this stuff," I say.

"Actually, I find it kind of interesting."

I hesitate once we arrive outside The Brass Rail. It seems dishonest to play along with him. "Um, Gavin? My mom got remarried here. I already know the ghost story about this place."

"Really? Do you know about Arthur's Tavern, too?"

"Haunted ladies' room upstairs? I've dragged my friends there twice."

Gavin sighs, sounding disappointed. He was happy to share this with me, and now I'm ruining the night for him. I can't think of a way to salvage the date.

"How about the ghost at the PATH station?" he asks.

I'm relieved that the story doesn't sound familiar. "Never heard of it."

He grins. "Great. Let's go."

We walk in silence for a bit before he asks, "What did you do today?"

"Actually, it's been a bad day." I can't bring myself to mention Oscar's illness without crying, but I manage to tell him about the handprints on my wall. "Blake was dog-sitting last night, so I was home alone. The whole thing doesn't make any sense. The apartment door was locked. And would a ghost use paint? I don't understand how my own hand was red."

"I'm sure there's a logical explanation. There must be something you're missing."

"That's pretty funny coming from the Haunted Hoboken tour guide," I joke. Still, I can't help shivering just thinking about this morning.

We stop at a light, waiting to cross the street. Gavin seems fidgety, glancing around, then fiddling with his bow tie. The light turns green.

"Wait," he says.

The traffic is clear. "What for?"

He answers by taking my hand and pulling me toward

him. His arms envelop me, and I feel safe for the first time in days. I lean into him. His lips graze my hair.

"I've missed you," he says.

I step back a little, look into his eyes, but he doesn't let go. Before I can answer, he kisses me. His lips are soft and warm. The summer heat is around me, dancing through me, until I'm tingling with joy.

"This is perfect," he whispers.

We kiss more, right on Washington Street, and there is no one else in the whole city except Gavin. Despite everything else, the happiness buoys me. His kiss is a mix of urgency and tenderness. When we stop, I need to catch my breath.

He takes my hand as we continue toward Hoboken Terminal. The commuters rush here and there, but I barely notice anything except his presence beside me.

We kiss again at the entrance, and it feels like a promise. No one has kissed me like Gavin. My mind races with plans and the future and the incredibleness of this night.

"The tour," he finally says.

"Right. The tour." He takes my hand and we leave the terminal through a tunnel that connects to the PATH. The subway area feels twenty degrees hotter. It even smells hot.

Without paying to go through the turnstiles, we're still close to the head of the tracks where the trains pull in. A subway arrives on track number 3 and stops with a sound that makes me think of a loud exhale. Gavin leads me to the middle track and points in the distance.

"I'll try to use my best dramatic voice." He coughs. "It was an August night when an off-duty train engineer spotted a young woman wandering on the track. She wore a long, pale dress which flowed as she moved. He called to her, but she wouldn't answer. Worried about her safety, he glanced around for someone to notify. When he turned back she was gone."

"Oooh."

"Several minutes later," Gavin continues, "he spotted her again on the otherwise empty platform. He approached her and politely asked if she was lost. When she didn't answer, he offered to accompany her home. 'It's too late to walk alone,' he told her. They exited the station side by side. They passed the Hotel Victor as he escorted her several blocks down Hudson Street. At one point, the sound of crying distracted him, and when he turned around, the woman had mysteriously vanished."

Gavin pauses as a train arrives with a whoosh of air. A train conductor makes some announcements. From where we stand, it's garbled except for the word "Hoboken."

"Let's sit outside," Gavin says. "Maybe there's a breeze. I'll finish the story there."

Exiting the station, we walk across the street to the bench by my apartment, the one Blake and I sat on ages ago when he first told me the truth about my dad. Gavin rests his arm across my shoulder, and I lean comfortably into him.

"Is this part of the tour?" I ask after he kisses me again.

"Only for you," he says.

"You were up to the part where the girl disappeared."

"Right. The man calls out, but doesn't see the girl again. Her disappearance troubles him. Where could she have gone? During the daylight hours, he returns to the house on Hudson Street where he last saw her and knocks on the door. An elderly woman answers, and he explains his dilemma. Does she know the girl? The woman starts to weep. She retreats into the house for a moment, but returns to the door with a faded photograph. 'Is this the girl you met?' she asks. He recognizes her right away. 'That's my sister, Adele,' she explains. 'She's been dead over two decades. First my parents, then her. When they passed suddenly, she started wandering aimlessly in her nightgown. Went a little crazy, she did. The last time she was seen alive was at the train station. They said she walked toward the oncoming train as if she never saw it. Died instantly. But you brought Adele home to me. Thank you.' The man realized he'd been in the presence of a ghost. After that, he would only work at the train station during the day."

"That's quite a story. It's almost like the plot to a movie. Hey, do you want to come in and we can rent one or something?" I don't want the night to end yet.

Gavin's phone buzzes, and he glances at a text. "I should be going. Sorry."

He walks me to the entrance of my building. We say good night, but there's a quickness to his kiss now, as if he's late, in a hurry.

The apartment is empty, but Blake left me a note saying it's his last night away. "Sorry," he scrawled at the bottom. Next to the paper is a vegan chocolate bar.

I eat the chocolate as I check the window locks. It's sad going to sleep without Oscar. There's a message on the home machine saying that he's resting comfortably. Thank goodness. I must have missed the vet's call when I was out with Gavin.

My mind replays Gavin's ghost story, which isn't as much fun now that I'm home alone for the night. I try to think about something wonderful, like kissing him, but that doesn't help me sleep. Would his parents like me? Would he get a car soon? I start to plot ways we can see each other during the school year. There must be a train to Parsippany. Maybe his town has a shelter or a vet's office where Mom or Stanley could drive me to volunteer. Gavin's cousin lives in Hoboken. Surely he must come back once in a while.

I run through our evening together. It was magical, but I can't help thinking that something changed at the end of the night.

I lie in bed thinking about kisses and handprints and trains. Uneasy, I get up and move a kitchen chair in front of the apartment door so no one can enter without rousing me. Finally, I decide to sleep on the couch, as far away from where the handprints appeared as possible. Feeling more at peace, I doze off.

I wake in the morning with a vague sense of unease. What

will I find today? I steel myself to check the walls, then the rest of the apartment, too. Everything is normal except for Oscar's absence. Relieved, I eat breakfast, shower, and get dressed for my shift at the bookstore.

Gavin calls just as I'm leaving. "Can I see you this morning?"

"I would love to, but I have work."

"Until when?" His tone sounds more distraught than eager.

"Two. What's the matter?"

"I really need to talk to you before then. Meet me on the bench?"

"When?"

"I'm already here." He sounds miserable. Something is definitely wrong.

# 19

# BREAKING

I agree to meet Gavin even though I'll be late to the bookstore and Henry will frown at me more than usual. I try to imagine a logical explanation for why Gavin seems unhappy. Maybe he needs to go back home sooner than expected. Or he just found out he has a contagious disease transmitted by kissing. I mean, he didn't meet someone else overnight, right?

I find Gavin standing by the bench. He pulls me close and holds me a moment, but the emotion is different this morning. The hug doesn't feel passionate. It feels like good-bye.

"What's going on?" I ask. "Tell me."

He holds me away from him, both hands on my arms.

"Don't . . . don't take it the wrong way. I really like you. But—"

I pull away from him. "You have a girlfriend at home?"

"No, it's not like that."

"I thought last night was great. Did I misread everything?"

"It *was* great. The best." He pauses. "I'm sorry I can't explain this better."

Suddenly Gavin is as mysterious as his ghost story. "Keep trying," I say.

"I . . . I can't see you anymore."

"Why not?"

He looks away. "I just can't."

I want to demand an explanation, to understand what's happened to turn the best night of my life into the worst morning. But I have my pride. I don't say anything, not a single word. As I turn and leave, there is no longing glance backward like in the movies.

A sob catches in my throat, but I take a deep breath and will myself not to cry. It was a few dates, nothing more. What was I thinking? That we were already soulmates? Ridiculous.

I can't show up to work crying. Needing some time to calm down, I detour through the park. This is a mistake. There are couples everywhere. Old couples holding hands, like they've been happily married for decades. A guy and girl I know from school, famous for their PDA. Young parents pushing a stroller. Finally, somewhere around Fourth Street, my sadness solidifies into anger.

What is wrong with Gavin? None of this makes any sense.

Forget him. He doesn't deserve me.

My phone rings and for a desperate moment I find myself hoping it's Gavin, that he's realized he made a terrible mistake. But it's Henry calling from the bookstore, no doubt wanting to know why I'm late.

"I'm on my way," I say.

"Good," Henry says. "Because we have a problem. We've been robbed."


I freeze at the entrance to the bookstore, unable to move, unable to speak.

The shop looks like someone let a rowdy group of toddlers run around unsupervised. Books litter the wooden floor and a display of stuffed animals has been toppled over.

"It was like this when you arrived?" I ask.

Henry nods. "The strange thing is, I checked the doors and windows, and there's no sign of a break-in."

"How is that possible?"

"I don't know, Ella."

I wander around the store in shock. He's right. There is no broken glass, no open windows. The store is a mess, but nothing is really damaged. It's more mischief than destruction. How did the thief enter? Another locked-room mystery, like the handprints on my wall. Someone had to get in, and then lock up on the way out.

Unless it was a ghost.

"Are there any handprints?" I ask.

"You mean fingerprints?"

"Never mind."

The register drawer is open, revealing empty slots where the cash used to be.

"It was like that when I got here," Henry says.

I try to estimate the amount of money that's been stolen. It must be several hundred dollars.

"We should call the police," Henry says.

He's right. I need to get my bearings first, though, to try to figure out what's going on. So many strange things have occurred over the past few days. The break-in must be connected.

I consider calling Grace for help. But no. After the handprint incident, I don't want to involve her. If she thought I was to blame for the painted prints, she would probably say something ridiculous, like I broke into the bookstore myself.

I inspect the damage more closely. Many of the displays look disheveled, but only certain sections of books have been pulled to the floor. The cat and kitten nonfiction has been dumped, along with the vegetarian cookbooks, and several books about Tarot readings and ghost stories. There has to be a connection between them.

Of course. It's *me*. All the books are somehow related to me. Why isn't the rest of the store messed up? I'm not sure what this means, but I don't want Henry to draw the same conclusion.

Away from the other books, I spot *The Collected Works of Edgar Allan Poe* sticking out from under a chair. Gavin and I talked about the Marie Rogêt story. No one else knew about that. It was the two of us, alone, on the Stevens campus.

It dawns on me. Ghosts don't need cash from the bookstore register. But someone who worked two jobs to save for a car does. Someone like Gavin.

# 20

# DAMAGE

Henry hovers by the phone, wanting to report the bookstore break-in. But if Gavin might somehow be involved, I need more time to think it through. If we call the cops and he admits to them that he's responsible . . . I'm not sure I can handle the idea of him being arrested.

"Don't call the police yet. They'll insist on contacting Mom," I say. "I don't want to ruin her last days of vacation."

Henry frowns in obvious disagreement. "Whoever did this must have a key. That's the only possible explanation."

Well, that rules out Gavin. Except . . .

A key. An image of Gavin at the hardware store duplicating the house key for Blake flashes through my mind. I left him to talk to Blake about the cat key holder. Gavin could have made extra copies for himself.

I need to call Gavin. I'll give him one chance to explain before we notify the police.

"Can you check the back area again and make sure nothing

is missing?" I ask Henry. He shakes his head, as if to say he already did that, but he leaves me alone. I only need a few minutes to make the call.

I dig for my phone inside my bag. My fingers brush a thick envelope. BENTON BOOKS is imprinted on the corner. The envelope is stuffed with cash.

*No.*

It has to be the money from the register. How did I possibly end up with it?

I think about my abrupt meeting with Gavin. He could have slipped the envelope into my bag this morning. But that doesn't make sense. There's no point in stealing the money, then giving it back right away. Unless he felt guilty.

We can't exactly call the police if there's no theft. Now that I'm unknowingly implicated . . . I can't let Henry learn what's going on. There has to be a way out of this mess. I stare at the money, deciding what my next move should be.

While Henry's in the back, I leave the envelope of cash on a shelf where he'll find it before I head to the employee bathroom to splash cold water on my face. I'm still in there when he yells for me.

"Ella! They didn't take the money after all!"

"Really?" I emerge with my best look of fake surprise.

"It's pure mischief!"

"What a relief." Before he can insist that we call the police anyway, I put the stuffed animals back in their carousel. "We should clean up," I say.

We finish straightening the books, working together but in different sections, before Henry finally retreats to the back room. Once he's out of earshot, I dial Gavin, but the call goes straight to voicemail. I hang up without leaving a message.

I'd really like to sit quietly and think, but I don't want to risk any questions from Henry. My head is pounding. I tackle the mail that's accumulated, needing to focus on the mundane, the practical. I throw out the junk, make a stack of bills for when Mom returns, and create a separate pile of book order packages from UPS.

The first package contains a flower gardening guide and a memoir written by a veterinarian. I enter the books into our inventory system and the name for the special order pops up: Henry. I finish processing them and put them aside for later. The next package is a bird-watching guide. I don't recognize the customer, but I leave him a message that his book is in. Grace's movie book has also arrived. I'll tell her later.

The last package is a heavy one, and I pull out two hard-covers: *Warning Signs: A Parent's Guide to Mental Illness* and *Heredity's Role in Mental Health*. The books are thick and look daunting. I enter them into the system. They are also a special order, and I blink a few times, as if that will change the name that appears on the screen.

Andrea Benton.

Mom had chosen them for herself. I close the screen quickly as if that will change the facts. I can't stop goose bumps from prickling my arms as I stare at the books she ordered. I open the first one, flip through the pages. As the truth sinks in, I can't focus on any actual words. I drop to my knees on the floor.

Mom purchased the books because of me. Because of Dad's secret illness and her fear that I'm unwell. Unwell enough to somehow leave handprints, as the red paint on my palm suggested. Unwell enough to hear a crying cat that isn't there, and to even trash the family bookstore without remembering. As the pieces fall into place, I stay on the floor, too weak to stand.

I'm in trouble.

# 21

# BETRAYAL

It had to be me. The handprints, the moved photo, the book-store break-in. I did these things. There's no other answer. Gavin isn't responsible. Neither is a ghost.

I can't let Henry know. Both of the books Mom ordered barely fit inside my messenger bag, but I succeed in cramming them in. I sink into one of the reading chairs, rubbing my temples. Henry finds me a little while later.

"You look ill." His usual frown is replaced with a crinkled expression of concern.

"I was taking care of the book orders, but my head started to ache." I hope to distract him from asking me more questions. "Two books came in for you. Gardening and a veterinarian memoir." It occurs to me that the memoir seems more like something Dad would read than Henry. I really don't know much about Henry. Then it hits me. Maybe he has information about Dad's illness that could help me figure all of this stuff out.

"You knew my father, right? Were you close?"

Henry is slow to answer. "We both loved animals," he finally says.

"Oh?" I wait, but he doesn't seem inclined to share more. It's too awkward to ask him directly about Dad's illness, but whatever Dad suffered from must be hereditary. Depression, bipolar disorder, schizophrenia. I know the terms but not enough to diagnose myself. I would need to resist the urge to search online later for my symptoms. Whatever disease it was, it put him in the hospital and maybe led to his death.

"If you're not feeling well, I could drive you to the doctor," Henry says.

"I just need to rest here for a few minutes."

"Are you sure you're okay?"

"I'll be all right."

Henry walks away. I close my eyes until his footsteps fade.

I have to hold on until Mom comes home. Less than forty-eight hours now. I missed her last call, but I can't try to reach her and pretend that everything is fine. I'll have Blake keep an eye on me so I don't do anything else stupid or hurt myself, like the girl who walked on the train tracks in Gavin's ghost story.

The thought of Gavin makes me want to puke. He'd been using me to pass the time, to amuse himself or something. He dumped me like people abandon a cat that claws the furniture.

Forget Gavin. I breathe deeply and pull out my phone. Blake answers right away and says to meet him at the café at Fifth and Washington in an hour. I don't tell him anything about my state of mind—that I swept books off shelves without remembering it. I'll wait until we are face to face.

My head spins. I consider calling the psychologist I used to see in middle school. Mom always made the appointments for me, but I find her number online and dial it. My heart is beating loudly enough that I'm afraid she'll hear it through the phone. But I only get the machine, saying she'll be out of the office until September and to call 911 if it's an emergency.

It's not that kind of emergency, so I call Grace instead, then Jana, but neither one answers. I don't bother to leave a message for them. I say good-bye to Henry and pretend that I'm going home. He agrees to take care of closing the store.

It's a long walk on Washington Street to meet Blake. My bag bulges with Mom's books, weighing me down. I wish he had picked someplace closer. Halfway there, I pass a burger place and glance inside like an onlooker at a car crash, inexplicably drawn to the fast-food beef horror.

Sitting inside is Gavin.

He's at the counter facing the street with a redheaded girl next to him. An extremely pretty redheaded girl. He doesn't notice me as he talks to her and eats his non-vegan meal. This particular burger place doesn't offer vegan-friendly alternatives—even the French fries are made with animal products. I should know. I've asked before.

I rush away before Gavin can see me, anger fueling my quickened stride. The last time I made spaghetti, the water boiled over, leaving a burnt smell in the kitchen and an ugly brown ring around the stove burner. That's what I think of now: boiling water. Ugly brown rings. The sizzling stovetop.

Somehow Gavin's meat-eating feels like more of a betrayal than his lame breakup and even his redheaded friend. Why lie about who he is? I didn't even tell him I was vegan. He brought it up—a happy surprise at the picnic lunch. He fooled me into liking him and then unceremoniously dumped me. It doesn't make any sense. Part of me wants to call him, to demand an explanation, or at least express my rage. Unless . . . Gavin never actually told me he was vegan. Maybe I imagined it, like the crying cat. I don't know what to believe anymore. What if my own memories can betray me? Is this how Dad felt before he was admitted?

I'm late to the café, but there's no sign of Blake.

"Do you need a table, Miss?" a waitress asks.

"Not yet, thank you. I'm waiting for someone." I'm too self-conscious to sit alone. I lean on the railing outside instead, inhaling the humid summer air, exhaling, trying to stay calm.

Many breaths later, Blake still hasn't shown. He doesn't answer my messages, either. I'm alternating between feeling awkward and angry when Grace calls.

"Want to get together?" she asks.

"Yes, that would be great." I need someone rational to talk to. "I thought you were mad at me. You left in such a huff yesterday."

"What are you talking about?" She sounds surprised.

"The handprints."

"I don't know what you mean, El."

"You came and looked at the handprints on my wall. Remember? I thought they were made of blood, but you realized they were paint."

"I'm sorry . . . you're not making sense."

*I feel like I'm sinking under water and I can't touch the bottom.*

"Grace, come on, you were there with me before you left all annoyed. I remember."

Her voice is gentle. "I don't think so. I think you're confused. Maybe . . ." She pauses. "Maybe you imagined it?"

*I reach my arms above the surface, but it's no use. My head is submerged, my body's too heavy.*

I try again. "Grace, I swear on the grave of my father that you were there. You were in my room with me yesterday morning."

"No. I'm sorry, Ella. Should I meet you? Where are you now?"

*I'm drowning.*

Nothing makes sense. Gavin, the lying non-vegan, dumps me. Mom, concerned about my mental health, purchases books to analyze me. I don't remember taking the bookstore money. I do remember Grace's visit, which apparently didn't happen.

My hands shake as I hang up without saying good-bye. I leave the restaurant in a daze. As I cross the street, a car blares its horn. I jump back to the curb. There's no warning from Dad this time to save me. Had there ever been a warning?

It's all too much. I can't distinguish between what's real and what's imagined. I could be suffering from delusions. Hallucinations. I hurry back to the apartment building and once inside, I drop my heavy bag on the counter. Oscar saunters over, meowing insistently. I lean down to rub him.

Oscar. But I left him at the vet's office. I took him to the vet, didn't I?

His fur brushes against my leg. Uncertainty wells up inside me. I choke back a scream.

# 22

# THE ACCIDENT

Blake rushes into the kitchen. "What's the matter?"

I cover my mouth with one hand, point at Oscar with the other.

"Oscar's doing much better," he says. "The vet left a message here that we could bring him home. I have some medicine for him, half a tablet twice a day. They said since they can't diagnose the exact cause, for now they'll just treat the symptoms." He stops talking, really looks at me. "Are you all right?"

I take my hand away from my mouth, but don't trust myself to speak. I nod instead.

"That's why I didn't meet you. Didn't you get my text?"

"No."

"Want to get something to eat now?"

"I'm not hungry. I . . . I'm not feeling well."

"Maybe you should rest."

Yes, rest. I'm clearly on edge. Oscar is better, with a perfectly logical explanation for his reappearance. I have him

and Blake to keep me company. I'll ask him about his relationship with Grace later, when I'm feeling calmer. I don't want to
think anymore right now. About Grace, about anything.

After a quick shower, I put on sleep shorts and a T-shirt
even though it's still early. I fall asleep quickly and the nap
lasts for hours.

When I wake, I'm reluctant to leave my bed and face the
world. I turn over the events from the last few days in my
mind. Grace said she wasn't here yesterday, but she was with
me in my room. She brought coffee. We took photos with my
phone. Proof! The photos would show that she's lying.

Except, now I can't find my phone.

I jump out of bed, check all of the usual places, but it
doesn't turn up. Mom would tell me to retrace my steps.
When's the last time I had it? I remember texting Blake from
the café, then talking to Grace. I could have left my phone
there. Or it could be lost in my room somewhere. I dial my
number from the landline but don't hear it ring.

Still determined to prove that Grace was here, I check the
kitchen trash for her coffee cup, but Blake must have emptied
the garbage. He's sitting on the couch watching more *Dumbest
Crooks Ever*.

"Have you seen my phone?"

"No. You think you threw it away?"

"Never mind." I search for another fifteen minutes. It will
turn up. It always does. Misplacing my phone is *not* a sign

of any mental problems. I get a glass of water and go back to bed with a contented Oscar purring next to me. I flip through one of the psychology books that Mom ordered, but reading about diseases makes me suddenly suspect that I might have symptoms of all of them.

Later, Blake comes into my room to see how I'm doing. I tuck the book under the covers.

"You look sick," he says. "Am I supposed to check for a fever or something?"

Before I can answer, he puts his lips on my forehead, lets them linger there. It feels . . . not quite brotherly. Am I imagining that, too?

In the morning, I'm relieved that nothing out of the ordinary happens. When I open my shade, the sun greets me. Oscar eats like his normal self. I only need to get through one more day until Mom returns. She'll be home by the time I wake up and everything will be all right again.

I'll wait until I can talk to Mom alone. She'll help me deal with finding a doctor, getting medicine, doing whatever I need to get well. Maybe she left me a message. I reach for the phone on my nightstand before I remember it's missing. I search the apartment one more time. Blake is in the kitchen staring at the nearly bare fridge.

"There's nothing good to eat. Want to go out for lunch?

That café has lots of vegetarian stuff. I'm sure they could make something vegan if you ask. Or do you want me to bring food home for you?"

I'm still worried about, well, everything, and I'm not in the mood to go out, but I don't want to be home alone. If I go with Blake, I could look for my phone at the café. That's the last place I remember using it. Even if I'm not hungry, at least it would help pass the time.

"I'm buying," he says. "Or rather, Stanley is. Let's splurge."

"Okay," I reluctantly agree.

We sit outside at a table covered by a big maroon umbrella. The conversation lags, and I'm overly aware of the many things that I don't want to talk about. I don't want to mention Gavin dumping me. I can't discuss Mom's book order. And I don't want to admit that I thought I was haunted before realizing it's actually some type of mental illness.

The waiter comes over and we order grilled vegetables on pita bread without cheese for me and some crab cake sliders for Blake.

I hear dripping and look at the sunny sky. It's not raining. I wrap my arms around myself before I realize that it's the overhead air-conditioning unit splotching the umbrella by my head. I need to calm down.

"What's the matter?" Blake asks.

"Nothing," I say. "I hope they have good weather for the flight home."

"You miss them?"

I can't even begin to talk about how much I need my mother right now, even if she did lie to me. "Yes. You?"

He shrugs. "Not so much. I'm kind of used to being on my own. My mother worked for years to support us, so she wasn't always around."

It seems like he wants to say more, but my brain won't formulate an encouraging response. I arrange my silverware precisely so that the fork and knife are parallel to each other. How will Stanley react to my mental problems? Will he be supportive if I need outside help? Mom will have to handle Stanley. Dealing with him is her territory. She'll get me whatever I need to heal.

"You seem burdened," Blake says. "That's the brother talking, not the future psych student. Anything you want to talk about?"

I scramble for the least problematic answer. "What's going on with you and Grace?"

"Nothing. Why?"

"You went to the beach together, right?"

"Yes, but it wasn't a big deal," he says.

"You and Grace are just friends?"

"She's my stepsister's BFF," he says with a smile. "Of course, we're friends. But that's all."

"That's not what she said. Why didn't you guys invite me to join you?"

"It was her idea to go, but it wasn't a date. You had someplace to be that afternoon. The animal shelter, I think."

We pause as the waiter brings our food.

"Look, it was a mistake to go with her," he says. "It seemed better not to say anything afterward. You've known Grace for years, but she doesn't seem like a good friend. I realized that day how jealous she is of you."

I push my food around on the plate. "I don't think so. What's to be jealous of?"

"You're prettier, for one. I bet you get better grades. You probably have your whole life mapped out—which classes you'll take for the next three years, which colleges you'll apply to for veterinary medicine, all that. And she's floundering a bit more, right? She probably can't make a career out of watching movies."

Even though I'm angry with Grace, it still stings to hear him criticize her. "You've got it all wrong. I'm the one who's floundering now. Grace and I . . . we have different ways of approaching things."

Blake gives me a knowing smile, as if he's wiser than I am. We don't talk much the rest of the meal. And despite a search while he pays the bill, my phone is nowhere to be found.

Back in the apartment, Blake spends time on his cell. I feel disconnected without mine, isolated from the world. I actually jump when the kitchen phone rings next to me. "Hello?" I answer.

A woman speaks in rapid French. At least, I think it's French. She's talking too fast for me to be sure.

"English," I interrupt. "Speak English!"

"*Non anglais*," she says and the deluge of foreign words begins again.

Blake stands, takes the phone from me. "Hello? *Je parle français*." He listens, begins to pace. "*Non*," he says softly. "*Non*." He listens some more. "*Êtes-vous certains?*" He covers his eyes with his hand for a moment. "*Je comprends*." He digs through the junk drawer, finds paper and a pen, jots something down.

"What is it?" I ask.

He turns away so I can't see his face. "*Oui, oui. Je comprends. Au revoir.*"

The way he moves, in slow motion, tells me it's bad news. Our parents are in Paris. A woman calls and speaks excitedly in French. Blake covers his face while they talk.

Something horrible has happened.

He won't look me in the eye after the phone call. "I think you should sit down," he says, as if a chair will make the news any more bearable.

"Tell me," I whisper.

"There's been an accident."

# 23

# UNCERTAIN

Blake explains something important to me, but it's like he's miles away instead of in our kitchen. I make out some of the words: Mom, Stanley, critical condition. I piece together enough to know that there's been a bad taxi accident involving our parents. Blake seems in as much shock as I am.

What if Mom dies? What if I never get to see her again?

The scream rises in my throat. If it erupts, I will never stop screaming. Never. I hold it in.

Blake's face is wet, and we hug, clinging to each other in desperation. He feels sturdy in my arms compared to the fragility of everything else. Life is fragile. Even my mind is fragile. I am flooded with anxiety, but it is hard to know how much is reaction to the news and how much is the illness that plagues me. I will have to tell Blake something is wrong with me. But not now. Concern for Mom and Stanley dwarfs my own issues.

"They're both hanging on, right?" I ask.

He nods as if speaking about it will make us break down. "We have to go to them."

"You're right," he says. "I'll look into flights."

While he checks flight times, I search for a suitcase. Mom brought our luggage on her honeymoon, but I find a large backpack and bring it into my bedroom.

"Good news," he calls to me. "There are two seats on a flight out of Newark tomorrow morning. Do you have your passport handy? I might need the number."

*A passport.* I don't have one. I've never traveled outside of the United States. Mom and I talked about getting me one when I left for college, in case I wanted to study abroad. We thought I had plenty of time to take care of all that.

I join Blake in the family room. "Is there any way to travel without it?"

"You don't have a passport?"

I shake my head slowly.

"That's a problem." He runs his hand through his hair. "You need it for Europe, El."

I slump onto the couch, struggling to hold myself together. "You should go without me. Someone should be there with them. What if they can't fly home right away? What if they need you to make medical decisions?"

He moves next to me, takes hold of my hand. We sit, numb and deathly quiet, until the phone rings. We both jump, but Blake gets there first. "Hello?" He listens for a few seconds before hanging up. "Sales call," he explains.

I'm tempted to rip the phone out of the wall. It will never ring again without reminding me of the woman calling—of that disastrous moment. I hate that I couldn't understand her. I hate the sound of the word *accident*. I hate everything.

"I need to get some air," Blake says. I'm tempted to beg him not to leave in case something happens to him, too. But I sit mutely. I don't even bother to lock the door behind him. No one can hurt me anymore. Nothing seems to matter.

The only thing that would make me feel better is seeing Mom. I decide to search online for expedited passports. There's a place in Manhattan that can do it in one business day. They're closed now for the weekend, but I can turn in the paperwork Monday morning when it reopens. It's expensive, but maybe we can charge it to Stanley's credit card.

When I hear Blake's key in the lock, I rush to meet him at the door. "I think I can get a passport in the city. Maybe we can fly out on Tuesday?"

"Good thinking," he says. "We can keep checking on Andrea and Stanley throughout the weekend. Maybe their condition will miraculously improve." He hands me a container of soup and a plastic spoon. "You have to eat."

*We need a miracle.* Is there something about their injuries that he's not telling me? "I'm not hungry."

"I know. But you need to eat a little. Please? Let me take care of you."

I'm too weary to argue. The soup tastes awful, but I swallow it anyway.

I want to know more about Mom. I want to ask about worst-case scenarios, about . . . I can't even formulate the questions.

"I'll call the hospital tomorrow," Blake says, as if he knows what I am thinking. "First thing in the morning, to get an update."

The soup container is empty—somehow I've managed to finish it. Blake sits next to me, puts his arm around my shoulders, and pulls me close so that my head rests on his chest. His heartbeat soothes me, and I close my eyes, trying to forget everything.

I feel him shudder, stifle a sob.

"It's all my fault," he whispers.

"What is?" I shift my head, catch his pained expression.

"I told Dad that they had to visit the Louvre. The chess set there from the Middle Ages—I told them to go. That's where they were headed in the taxi. The woman said they were on the way to the museum when . . ." He can't finish.

"It's not your fault," I say. Our faces are inches away from each other, and I can see the torment etched in his eyes.

"If only—"

"We're thousands of miles away. We couldn't cause this. Or prevent it."

"You really think so?"

I nod. "We'll get through this somehow." I need to convince him and myself, too.

"Thank you." Blake strokes my palm. His fingers trail up my bare arm in slow motion, across the inside of my elbow, my collarbone, my throat. When he gets to my face, he brushes his index finger gently across my lower lip, back and forth.

I can barely breathe, barely understand what this means. I stop his hand with my own. He locks eyes with me as he intertwines our fingers, leads my hand to his cheek.

"Blake—"

He leans in and kisses me. His lips are confident on mine, certain.

I can't think. My brain stops comprehending as my eyes flutter closed.

He wraps his arms around me. His kiss becomes more insistent, a gust of wind before the hurricane.

I don't move away, but I don't kiss him back, either. I'm trapped in some type of nightmare where nothing makes sense, nothing matters. I need time to think, but it's like his mouth has short-circuited my mind.

He moves his lips to my shoulder, then from my shoulder to my neck, slowly, slowly, up to my ear.

A moan escapes from me. I'm paralyzed with indecision. This is wrong.

His breath is warm in my ear. "Please," he whispers. "Please. I need you. You're the only one who understands."

I shiver. We share so much in this moment. The worry. The indescribable fear of what we might lose.

But I can't do this.

He must realize it, too, because when I stand, he lets me go.

I scoop Oscar in my arms and take him to my room. I don't even bother to wash my face or brush my teeth. I collapse on my bed. Sleep is the only escape from all the confusion.

When I wake Sunday morning, my head pounds. I lie in bed with my eyes closed. It comes to me slowly, in fragments, as if the whole scenario is too much to process all at once.

Mom is hospitalized. But she can't be dead, right? I would feel her absence if she were gone.

I need to find the necessary documents and fill out the forms for my passport. After Blake speaks to the hospital, we should make the travel arrangements.

Blake.

There's something about last night. Blake's kiss. I need to talk to him, explain it was a misunderstanding. The anxiety made us act irrationally.

Pain hammers into my forehead, and for a minute, I actually care. I want to tell Mom I have the worst headache of my life, to ask her what to do. Then I remember all over again.

I wipe at my useless tears. When I open my eyes, my hands are red. Blood red. I stare at them as if they belong to someone else. This time I know it isn't paint.

Blood is everywhere. My hands, the sheets, Oscar's fur.

His body stays limp when I lift him.

Oscar is dead.

# 24

# SAYING GOOD-BYE

As I bolt from bed, I bump the nightstand and send my lamp crashing to the ground. Blake bursts into my room. "El!" His eyes widen. "What happened?"

"I don't know, I don't know." I hold Oscar's body in my blood-covered hands. "I can't remember anything. I woke up like this. Is he really dead?"

The room smells like my sweat, my fear.

Blake takes Oscar gently in his arms, places a hand on my cat's coffee-colored chest. He doesn't say anything. He doesn't have to. There must not be a heartbeat.

Staring at Oscar in horror, I yearn for my mother. I want her presence, a comforting hug, her calm voice telling me everything will be all right. Because I have a feeling nothing will ever feel all right again. I've crossed over into someplace permanently terrifying.

Blake doesn't seem to know what to do. After all his weird affection last night, he's standing three feet away and spouting a bunch of psychological phrases. I catch post-traumatic stress disorder, severe anxious reaction.

I'm trying to create some semblance of rational thought and his amateur psychology is not helping. "Shut up, Blake! Just shut up!"

"No. You killed your beloved pet in some sort of fugue state. You need medical help."

I process this, trying to think of an argument against it. I look at Oscar—the body of Oscar the Second.

"Maybe in France, after I see Mom. We need to make flight reservations. We—"

"El, you can't get on a plane in this condition. You need some type of psychiatric assessment, maybe medication." He pauses, giving me a chance to absorb this. "Why don't you get cleaned up, then we'll figure out what to do."

Cradling Oscar, Blake backs out of the room as if he's afraid of me.

I grab some clothes—no cat T-shirt, I can't bear a cat T-shirt—and turn on the shower. My image in the bathroom mirror is barely recognizable. Circles rim my eyes as if I was on the losing end of a fistfight. Blood covers my hands. The blood is even in my hair, clumping strands of it together in a gory mess.

Clutching my stomach, I heave beneath the shower spray. Nothing comes up. I close my eyes as the water runs crimson down the drain. My thoughts are incoherent. Only two steady refrains circle through my mind: *Mom is hurt. I killed*

*Oscar. Mom is hurt. I killed Oscar.* Then somehow it merges into *I killed Mom.*

No, she was injured in a car crash in Paris. I did not kill her. I struggle to keep the facts straight. It feels like my hold on reality is tenuous. I have to remember what happened—what I actually did.

Oscar. Poor Oscar. I thought I shared Dad's love of animals. But maybe I shared some of his mental instability as well. I scrub myself clean with soap and shampoo and more soap until the water rinses clear. I'm reluctant to leave the comfort of the shower, to face the most dismal day of my life.

Could I be that sick? Sick enough to hurt my pet? I trace my spiral out of control: ever since Mom and Stanley left, and the handprints appeared, and Gavin liked me then didn't, and I lost my phone, and Mom bought books about the hereditary nature of mental illness.

"El, are you okay in there?"

I turn off the water in response.

If only I could stop thinking and quiet the noises in my head. I hum to drown out the sound. Anything to make it stop.

I emerge into the kitchen, clean and dressed in shorts and a plain T-shirt.

"You're humming?" Blake stares at me.

I don't bother to answer him, because I can't explain about the refrain in my head. I can't explain anything.

"I called the hospital," he says.

"Are they doing any better?"

"Not the Paris hospital. A hospital for you."

"You need to call Paris," I say.

"I will. About the other hospital—I'm not technically your legal guardian, but if you describe what happened, how you're feeling, they'll admit you. What do you think?"

Legal guardian. If Mom dies, I will need a guardian. The thought's too complicated to process. I rub my eyes, ignore his question.

"They can help you, El. Should we go there?"

I'm about to argue when I catch sight of Oscar's water bowl on the floor. "Yes, I'll go. But you have to get an update about Mom and Stanley first."

"Okay." He takes a crumpled paper from his back pocket and calls the number.

I pace around the apartment chanting *please, please, please* silently in my head as Blake speaks French in a low, calm voice. Please let Mom be all right. Please let her come home. Please let me be okay, too.

Blake hangs up. He's silent for a moment, as if composing himself.

"Tell me."

He sighs. "They're not sure how long they'll have to stay in the hospital. Stanley has a broken leg. He's on a lot of pain medicine, and they wouldn't let me speak to him yet. Your mom . . . she's unconscious, but they said she's stable."

"She's unconscious? Like in a coma?"

"I couldn't understand all of the medical terms. According to the person I spoke to, it seems they both are improving."

"You should still fly there without me. You can leave today."

Blake looks torn. "I don't think you should be alone right now. Is there anyone you can call?"

I silently run through a short list of friends and distant relatives. "Not really."

"I need to be here with you, then. At least until you see a doctor. Why don't you pack a few things? In case they want you to stay for observation."

I stall. *Stay for observation* sounds like a euphemism. "My room. There's so much blood. I can't go in there. Not yet."

"Sit," he says, guiding me into the kitchen chair near Oscar's water dish.

"Where's Oscar?"

"He's . . . I took care of it, for now. I can bring him to the vet later if you want them to handle his remains."

*His remains.*

"I'll take a quick shower. Then we'll come up with a plan."

"All right."

The bathroom door clicks closed behind him.

"All right," I repeat to no one. I imagine I hear Oscar meow weakly in agreement. *Poor Oscar.*

I need to pack, but it requires too much energy to move.

Motionless, I listen to the sound of the water running, the clock ticking. I memorize the details of the kitchen, as if I'll never be back here again.

Blake's phone charges in a nearby outlet. I miss my phone. I wonder if he has any old messages from Mom or Stanley. I would give anything to hear Mom's voice. What if I never get to talk to her again?

No. I can't let the fear consume me. I need to regain some type of control over this whole situation. I need to make arrangements for the store and find out more information about Mom's health. As much as I don't want to talk to Henry, I unplug Blake's phone and call the bookstore anyway.

"It's El," I say when he answers.

"I'm glad you called," Henry says. "A boy with bluish hair stopped in. He asked when your stepbrother would be moving to college. I offered to give you a message, but he said to wait until Blake was gone, then to tell you to call him."

Gavin. It all sounds odd but I can't focus on that—him—now. I break the news to Henry about Mom's accident. "I'll let you know as soon as I have more information. Once I get the hospital phone number, maybe you could call and check on her."

"Of course." Henry's voice shakes. "This is horrible, but I'll make sure the store continues to run smoothly. Let me know if there's anything else I can do."

After we hang up, I sit staring at the phone as the minutes

tick by, thinking about Gavin. I don't know why he would care when Blake leaves. I decide to call him, one last time.

Then I realize that his cell number is lost with my phone. I find the number for the hardware store and call with trembling hands, ready to hang up if anyone but Gavin answers. I can't deal with speaking to anyone else. I'm not even sure what to say to him.

He answers on the second ring.

"Blake?" he says. "I don't have anything left to discuss. I did what you asked. I'm done."

He thinks it's Blake since I called from his phone. I'm silent as I try to figure out what he is referring to.

Gavin rushes on. "El doesn't deserve any of this. I never should have let you talk me into dating her."

My mouth falls open. I'm speechless. Blake talked *me* into dating Gavin, not the other way around. We had a whole conversation about taking risks before he bet me money that we'd go out.

"Then, when I actually like her, what do you do? You make me break it off. I don't know what else you want from me, but I won't do this anymore."

He pauses, and I finally find my voice. "Gavin? It's El. I'm using Blake's phone. What's going on?"

"I—oh, El, I'm sorry. I've wanted to tell you the whole story. But you wouldn't return my calls."

"I lost my phone." The shower turns off. Blake will be

out any second. "I have to go," I whisper. I hang up, jam the phone back into the charger.

I need to stall Blake. After he goes into his room, I rush to the empty bathroom. He finds me kneeling in front of the toilet a few minutes later.

"Are you still feeling sick?" His voice sounds genuinely kind. At least I think it's kindness. I'm not sure anymore.

My head spins. Gavin had no reason to lie on the phone. He didn't even know it was me on the other end at first. I can't let Blake take me to the doctor yet. I need to figure this out. It's like putting together a puzzle after Oscar swats away some of the pieces.

"We should go soon," he says.

Wrapping my arms around my stomach, I moan. "I might throw up." Sweat beads across my forehead. The fact I'm a nervous liar helps me for once. The perspiration makes me look like a genuine puking person. "The car . . . I can't—"

"It's all right. Rest here for a few minutes. I'll bring you a glass of water."

I finally managed to tell him a convincing lie.

If I could only unravel the fiction from the facts. Blake manipulated Gavin and me, pushing us together, then pulling us apart. Why set up the whole relationship to hurt me? He must have realized how painful that would be.

Not as painful as losing Oscar, though. I adored that cat. I loved when he curled against me, romped through the apartment, purred in contentment. He was such an important part of my day, of my life.

Now I know. I could not have killed Oscar. I can feel the truth in my aching gut and the realization is like freedom. I would never hurt him.

Which only leaves one possibility. Blake killed Oscar to cause me pain, the same way he had Gavin break up with me. It sounds fantastical, and yet, it's the only logical answer.

Why ruin my life? I don't understand his reason for doing this. What exactly is he trying to accomplish?

Maybe he wants me to be weak, to be needy. To need *him*.

Last night. The kiss. Could it be a game of seduction for him?

Blake returns with the glass of water and his phone. I can't take the chance he'll see the call history, because then he'll know I spoke with Gavin. He'll realize that I figured out part of his plan, whatever it might be.

I think of Oscar's bloody body and start to dry heave.

Blake rushes to my side, brushes the sweaty hair from my forehead. He's tender in an awkward way, like he's not sure what to do next. For once. Because he certainly seemed to have everything else planned.

"I have some medicine that will make you sleepy," Blake says. "When you wake up, the car ride will be over. What do you think?"

*I have to stall.*

"You're right about going to the hospital. I need to get help. I feel so confused."

He rubs my back, soft caresses.

I know what I need to do.

# 25

# NINE LIVES

"I'm lucky you're here, Blake. What would I do without you?"

When I stand, I don't need to fake the wobble, because the nausea is real: nausea about what he did, about what comes next. Unsteady, I move closer and wrap my arms loosely around him.

He pulls me in and hugs me with a frightening fierceness.

"I'm so scared." The truth in my voice is convincing. I burrow my face into his chest as I hug him back. My stomach squeezes in repulsion.

I must do this.

I run my hands slowly down to his hips. He strokes my hair as I keep my face pressed against him. He lifts my chin, kissing me harder than last night. I kiss him back, forcing myself to respond with some type of passion.

*Survival. It's survival.*

I pull away as soon as I can. "I'm so glad you're here to help me. I don't know what I would do alone." I pause, wanting him to believe that he's won. "I don't want to leave yet. I want to pretend that everything's normal for a little longer. Can we stay awhile? Together?"

Blake scoops me up, carries me to the couch. Then he's on top of me, tugging at my clothes. Everything's happening way too fast. I need to slow him down.

"We could go to my bedroom." I drop my voice to a whisper. "No one's ever been in my bed. If it wasn't for all the blood . . . Let me clean up in there for a minute."

"It doesn't need to be clean, El. That doesn't matter."

"It matters to *me*. This has to be special."

He moves from on top of me. In the safety of my room, I lean against the closed door with my cat collage crumpled against my back. I choke back a sob so he won't hear me.

If I could get him out of the apartment for even a few minutes, I could escape. But any excuse I can think of will spoil the romantic moment and make him suspicious. He has to believe I'm swept off my feet. Even this delay is risky.

In a flurry, I rip off my sheets, trying not to think too long about the source of the blood on my bed. I wrap the bedding in a bundle and emerge to face him in the kitchen.

"Are you ready?" he asks.

His shirt is unbuttoned, and he moves closer to kiss me again, but I keep the sheets between us. I hope he interprets my shudder as anticipation. Behind him, I spot his keys hanging on the cat rack. His keys. If I can get him out of the apartment . . .

"One last favor." I smile. "Throw these in the wash?"

"You've got to be kidding me," he says, but he takes them from my arms.

"It sounds crazy, but I'll always remember this. The first time needs to be perfect. When you come back, I'll be ready. Please?"

He sighs, exasperated. "Promise?"

"Yes."

Blake piles sheets, detergent, and a baggie of quarters into the laundry basket. "I always take good care of you, don't I?"

I nod, not trusting myself to speak. *Leave. Hurry up and leave.*

The minute the door closes I make sure it's locked. He can't get back into the apartment without his keys. It's the best thing that's happened all day.

I don't have a plan—a real plan—other than to escape. There's no way he's washing the bloody sheets. He's probably dumping them in the trash instead, so there isn't much time.

My panicky brain won't think clearly. I stuff an HACC sweatshirt, my book, whatever is in reach into the backpack. *Focus.* I grab his phone, my wallet, my keys. There's some evidence I should be taking, too. I rush into Blake's room, rummage around. Inside the nightstand drawer I find a prescription bottle for Zoey Hill. Is it dog medicine? Never mind. I don't need that. What else should I take?

A cat cries faintly. I stop moving, afraid that it's my imagination. He cries again.

*Oscar.*

I fling open the doors to Blake's closet. Oscar rustles inside his carrier. He's still alive! I want to check how badly he's hurt, but it'll have to wait. I leave Oscar inside and carry him into the kitchen.

The elevator opens in the hallway. Blake rattles the doorknob, and I freeze as if he can see me somehow, as if he can reach through the door and touch me.

"It's me," he says. "Let me in."

I throw his keys into my bag and open the window to the fire escape. My head spins. Ugh. Now is not the time to feel woozy. Holding Oscar's carrier makes the descent impossible. I need both hands to climb.

"El? What's going on?"

I dump the random crap I'd packed onto the floor, keeping only the phone, wallet, and keys. Gently, I lift Oscar out of the carrier. I wrap him in the sweatshirt and place him inside the backpack, zipping it most of the way so he can't climb out. He gives one weak meow in protest.

"It's only for a few minutes," I promise him.

Blake pounds on the door and the loudness makes me jump.

Time to go.

I take a deep breath, strap the backpack across my chest, then open the window. Blake's still calling my name as I put one leg over the ledge.

# 26

# SHELTER

When I reach the street, there's no sign of Blake. I flag down a taxi and hop in the back. I need to get Oscar to the vet. It feels like déjà vu.

"Washington and Sixth, please."

As the cab drives away, I glance back. I hope Blake hasn't figured out that I'm gone. He might be worried that I'm not answering the door.

*Yeah, right.*

I spend the car ride rubbing the top of Oscar's head, trying to calm both of us. I can't tell the extent of his injuries, but he's definitely sleepy, as if he were drugged.

After I pay and get out at the vet's office, I realize my mistake. Blake will easily figure out my destination. The vet is an obvious guess, because he knows keeping Oscar safe is my top priority. Blake had already convinced the doctors to release Oscar to him once. I couldn't take the chance they would do it again.

*Think, think.* I have to take Oscar someplace else.

The animal shelter! They would let me leave him temporarily, and he could get medical care there, too. I turn off Washington and hurry toward Hudson. It's less crowded, so it will be easier to notice if I'm followed. I don't slow my pace until I'm safely inside the shelter.

Sneaking into the bathroom, I wash the blood off Oscar despite his meowing protests. I can't find an actual wound, but there's no time for a thorough exam. Once he's clean, I take a damp Oscar to Skyler and give her a condensed almost-true version of my dilemma: My parents are away and my stepbrother despises cats. I'm afraid he's been hurting him, and I need to keep him safe for a few days.

"The doctor's due here soon. I'll have him check Oscar out," she says. "We'll keep him in cattery two with a 'not available' sign. Cage eight is empty. I'll let the staff know he's yours."

Eight. My lucky number.

"I'll call your cell if we need you," she says.

"I lost my cell." Who can the shelter call? I can't use my home number, in case Blake manages to get back into the apartment. I'm not sure whose side Grace is on. I don't remember Gavin's cell number. Wait—it's programmed into Blake's phone.

"Call my friend Gavin." I give her the number. He's my only option.

"We'll take good care of Oscar," Skyler promises.

"Thank you for helping me." I give Oscar a kiss before putting him in her arms. I turn to go before I can change my mind about leaving him.

Outside the shelter, sweat drenches my armpits, a combination of summer heat, exertion, fear. I see a woman who looks like Mom and pain rips through me.

I will get to Paris soon, I promise myself. For now, I need to find someplace safe to stay. The bookstore feels like my only option. I could use Blake's phone to call Henry before I show up in my unraveled state.

Blake's phone. I pause for a minute, wondering what I can learn from it. He had Gavin's number. Who else's? I scroll through: Me. Gavin. Grace. His mom. Stanley. Zoey. Wasn't that the dog he looked after? It must be the number for Zoey's owner.

He cleared his texts but not his photos. I skim through a few of the ocean. The next one makes me gasp.

It's a photo of the muddy handprint I left on Dad's grave. Blake must have followed me to the cemetery before he left for the beach with Grace. Why would he take a picture of that?

Blake's phone rings in my hand and I jump, nearly dropping it. The caller ID says it's Gavin. I answer but hesitate before speaking.

"Hello?" Gavin sounds uncertain. He must be worried Blake might answer.

"It's me," I say.

"Where are you?" he asks.

The hairs on my arms stand up. I imagine Blake standing right behind him, telling him what to say, trying to find me.

"I can't tell you. But I have to get away from him."

"I left work early. I'm home. You can come here."

"I'm not sure who to trust right now."

He sighs. "I can explain. Can we meet somewhere?"

The phone beeps. Call waiting? No, I don't see anything about another call. Blake is clever, though. Could he find a way to track me through his phone?

*Oh no.*

If he has a find-my-phone app, he can pinpoint my location. My exact location. Paranoia kicks in, and I'm afraid to even mention a specific place to meet. "The Poe story," I say. "Meet me by the murder." I jog a block in the opposite direction before popping the phone battery out. Hoping he won't realize I'm near the shelter, I throw his phone into the Hudson and watch it sink.

# 27

# ABOVE

If Blake tracked me using his phone, he could be here in ten minutes. I'm torn about meeting Gavin, but I don't have a better plan. I head toward Sybil's Cave, trying to reconstruct a timeline of all the disturbing events.

The first incident: the muddy handprint on the bathroom mirror. Blake could have followed me to the cemetery, I guess. But he had lost his keys and couldn't get into the apartment. At least that's what he said. If he lied about that, he could have gotten in and left the handprint. But how would he have time to do all that and get to the beach and back?

The second incident: the handprint on the laundry room wall. I left my wash when Blake and I went to copy my keys. He was with me at the store. Even when he was browsing, he was never out of sight long enough. Did he have an accomplice? Grace? Gavin? But Gavin was with us at the hardware store, too. I don't know how Blake could have pulled that off.

Next: the handprints on my wall. Blake didn't sleep at

home that night. Wouldn't I have heard him come in the apartment? I think about the pill bottle. Could he have drugged me? We didn't eat together. But we did drink the smoothies he brought home, and later, I was exhausted.

Then there was last night. Poor Oscar. I don't even want to know where the blood came from. I'm grateful Blake didn't actually harm him.

Yet.

I shudder. I don't know if he wanted to seduce me, drive me insane, or both. Yet he was so thoughtful, helping the homeless man, shopping for Mom's gift, buying me the yellow dress. He fooled me into believing he was kind and caring.

Even if my dad's mental illness inspired Blake to make me feel crazy, I still don't understand *why*. I suppose if I'm ruled mentally incompetent, if Mom and Stanley were to die, he might control the insurance money and the bookstore. But even his evil-planning-genius couldn't cause a car crash in Paris. I had to hang on to the hope that they'd make it through this.

On the other side of Sinatra Drive, Gavin waits at the small park marked with a touristy Sybil's Cave sign. To my right, the Hudson shimmers. A few people jog by. It's not isolated but not so crowded that Blake could blend in.

I take a deep breath and cross the street to the metal arch. "Hey."

Gavin closes the gap between us. In two strides, he's right in front of me, giving me apologetic puppy eyes.

I step back to create space. "Explain."

He's silent for a moment as he glances around, and I wonder if he's looking for Blake, too. "Let's go to my apartment. We can talk on the way."

"I want to talk in public."

"I feel like he could be watching us."

Giving in, I suppress a shudder. I can trust Gavin, right? With a sense of dread, I realize I don't have much choice. I launch into my main question as we walk. "When I called from Blake's phone and you thought it was him, you said you did what he asked—that he told you to date me. What was that all about?"

He sighs. "I'll tell you, I promise. You go first. What's going on?"

"Our parents are seriously hurt." I keep my eyes focused straight ahead. "A car accident in Paris."

"El, I'm so sorry. Will they be all right?"

If I look at him, see the sympathy on his face, I'll completely lose it. "I hope so. I need to get away from Blake first. Then I can figure out how to get to my mother. Once I'm safe."

I tell him how Blake has been manipulating me, how I woke up thinking Oscar was dead. I watch his reaction carefully, trying to gauge his involvement.

"That's awful." Gavin seems sincerely shocked.

"At least he didn't really kill him. I left him at the shelter, but I gave them your number in case of an emergency."

He nods solemnly.

We reach the building where Grace and I had the psychic reading. The blue neon sign still glows. "Why are we stopping here?" I ask.

He points to the windows above the shop. "This is where my cousin lives."

"You live above the psychic?"

"Yes. We should get inside in case Blake is nearby."

"It's not like he'd be hanging around your building."

Gavin presses his lips together. "I can help you. I'll tell you what I know." He motions to the steps leading up to the door.

I pause as the realization sinks in. Gavin lives above the place where I had my Tarot reading. He is literally offering me help from above. The psychic was right. Not in the way that I expected, but still. I feel less like a lamb being led to slaughter as I follow him inside.

# 28

# LIES: PART I

The apartment Gavin shares with his cousin is railroad-style, with one room behind the other in a straight line. The pull-out couch in the living room is opened into a bed and there's a bookshelf against the wall filled half with books, half with folded clothes. From this first room, I can see a kitchen, followed by a bedroom.

"Home sweet home." He sits at the kitchen table, motions for me to sit next to him.

"It's your turn now," I say. "How did you meet Blake?"

"He was visiting my cousin." He takes a deep breath. "Listen. Blake told me that he had a stepsister with low self-esteem and that he wanted to boost her spirits. It seemed deceitful, and I wasn't interested. Then he showed me your picture and said . . . he said he would pay me. I was to show up at the bookstore and buy cat books, then visit you at the shelter a few times. After that, he said it was up to me."

Nausea passes over me like an ocean wave. "How much money did . . ." I swallow. "Never mind. I don't want to know."

"It gets worse." He stares at the floor.

"How is that possible?"

"He kind of gave me information about everything you like. So the odds of us connecting would be better, he said."

"Like what?"

"The vegan food. Your favorite sorbet flavor. The memoir you were reading. Obviously, your love of cats."

I'd like to storm out in a fit of rage, but honestly, it's all too much. I can barely move.

"I know it sounds awful, El. I shouldn't have done it, shouldn't have pretended to be someone different. I'm not a vegan guy looking to adopt a kitten. I'm sorry that I deceived you."

Gavin could have been Blake's accomplice in tricking me. If he showed Gavin the photo from the cemetery . . . but no, I was with Gavin and Blake when the handprint appeared in the laundry room.

"Don't even bother apologizing." I finally summon my energy and stand, grasping the chair so he can't see my unsteadiness. I hate having been so trusting, so easily duped. I feel like I need another shower.

"Wait," he says. "The thing is, I *did* like you. I still do. I mean, the setup was fake. But once I got to know you . . . I gave back the money to Blake. All of it. I told him I wouldn't trick you anymore, like with the cat noises. He was furious."

I stand perfectly still, like an unstable bomb that might detonate with the smallest hint of motion. I drop my voice to a whisper. "What about the cat noises?"

Gavin covers his eyes with his hand. "I didn't realize what

he was doing—the extent of it. He said it was a joke, planting the recording of that cat meowing near our picnic area. He told me to deny hearing anything. After the ghost tour, our kiss . . . the next morning, I told him no more. I let him know how I felt about you. But I was trapped. He said if I didn't do what he wanted, he'd reveal the whole story about how I was a pretend boyfriend who didn't really care."

Gavin stops, sighs deeply.

"Poor you." I don't try to hide my disdain. "What exactly did he want you to do?"

"On Friday, he told me to break up with you. Before noon."

"That's why you dumped me?"

"I thought . . . I thought once he was away at school, I'd contact you again. Maybe you'd get the message from the old man at the bookstore and you'd call me. I was hoping that if Blake never told you the truth, maybe we could get back together. I've been miserable since Friday morning. But I couldn't lie to you anymore."

"Is that all? Did you lie about anything else?"

Gavin shakes his head.

I don't know who I want to strangle more: Blake or Gavin.

"I really am sorry. About everything." He gets up, looks like he's about to touch me. I glare at him, and he steps away. "How about something cold to drink?" he asks.

Next to the sink, clean dishes are stacked on a draining rack. I suddenly remember when I was little, Mom washing dishes and teaching me to dry them. I complained it was unfair that the washer finished chores first, and she explained that the dishwasher also had to wipe the table. Everyone finished at the same time. Just like that, life returned to being reasonable.

Now nothing feels like it will ever seem reasonable again. I'm in denial, listening to Gavin unravel the past days, lie by lie.

The tears come. I can't hold them back anymore.

"Bathroom?"

He points and I rush through the door, not wanting him to see me fall apart. I run the water so he can't hear me sob. When I can finally breathe normally, I turn off the faucet and blot my eyes with a tissue. I toss it in the trash, where it lands on an empty bottle of red paint.

I storm into the kitchen, clutching the paint. "What is this?"

Gavin looks at me with sad eyes. "I was getting to that part."

"What part? You told me that was all the lies!" I squeeze the empty bottle with all my might.

"All of *my* lies," Gavin says. "But my cousin will be home soon to explain the rest."

The kitchen feels stuffy, like the air is made of cotton. Dizziness overcomes me and I sway.

Gavin has closed up the bed. He guides me to the couch, turns on the ceiling fan. He sits next to me, but not too close. I breathe with my eyes closed for a few minutes.

The last piece. That's how Blake managed the handprints. He duped someone else into helping him.

The key turns in the front door. A tall, redheaded girl saunters into the apartment.

"El, this is my cousin, Zoey." He pauses. "She's Blake's girlfriend."

# 29

# LIES: PART II

I blink, trying to comprehend the redhead in front of me. Gavin's cousin is a girl.

"Excuse me, but I'm not Blake's girlfriend anymore," Zoey says. "I'm his ex. As soon as I can find him to break the news."

I recognize her—she sat next to Gavin at the burger place. Her name sounds familiar, too. Blake said he was sleeping at a friend's to take care of a dog named Zoey. Of course! The pet-sitting was another lie. I could guess where he'd been sleeping.

"When did you decide to dump him?" Gavin asks.

"After I saw him kissing someone else."

She means me, of course. I'm about to explain how our kiss was meant to be a distraction, a way to get him off his game, when she holds up a picture on her phone. It's Blake and Grace, with Grace staring up at him like she's completely in love.

I gape at the photo. Grace was telling me the truth about her and Blake. Is there anything of mine he hasn't touched, hasn't ruined? Since he arrived, everything has gone wrong.

"How long were you dating?" I ask.

Zoey pours herself an iced tea, takes a long drink, but doesn't sit. She paces, her heels clicking across the wood floor. "About six months, since he flew into Newark. I met him when he filed a complaint at the airline where I work in customer service. Later, he admitted he made it all up as an excuse to meet. I was flattered at first, before I realized he loved manipulation more than he loved me. People don't matter to him much. You're either useful or not. And I was very useful."

"Blake was in New Jersey six months ago? That was when we were supposed to have our family dinner, but Blake never showed. Why would he fly all the way out here and not come to the restaurant?"

Zoey smiles, but it's more devious than cheerful. "He did go to the restaurant, actually. A fancy place, right? The three of you were already sitting down, laughing, having a great time without him. He was incredibly pissed off."

"So, you helped him play tricks on me just because he was angry?"

"He told me about how you dated his best friend and then cheated on him. He was getting back at you for what you did. Revenge."

"What? That's a total lie!"

"I didn't understand what he was up to until Gavin and I had a long talk. Besides, Blake told me that faxing papers and leaving handprints were simple pranks."

It falls into place—Zoey was Blake's accomplice. She could leave the handprint on the mirror while he was at beach and go to the laundry room while we were at the hardware store. It's a lot to take in.

"Wait . . . faxing what papers?"

"I don't know," she says. "Some records that were supposed to come from a psychiatric hospital."

"The hospital sent proof of my dad's real cause of death. You're telling me that wasn't real?" I'm dangerously close to bursting into tears again.

Zoey shrugs.

Mom told the truth after all. I've been so angry with her, but Blake was deceiving me the whole time.

# 30

# TANGLED WEB

Zoey's apartment feels uncomfortably warm as this new information sinks in. If Blake faked my father's mental illness, Dad is still the same man that Mom always described. It's mind boggling. Nothing has really changed over the past few weeks, just my perception swinging from one idea to the next. *Dad suffering from illness. Mom as a liar. Blake as a stepbrother who cared about me.*

I feel like someone opened the door on me while I was changing clothes. Naked. Foolish. I have a hard time unraveling all the layers of deception. Blake made me think my dad had a breakdown so I'd be more susceptible to feeling mentally ill myself. Then he proceeded to make me feel exactly like I was going insane.

Gavin is quiet as Zoey continues to pace. I'm sure they have more information. I decide to throw out ideas about all the strange occurrences to see what they'll reveal.

"The day the bookstore was trashed. I don't know when he got a key, but he threw books all over the floor."

"I copied all your keys for Blake when you visited the hardware store," Gavin admits. "You were down the aisle talking to him."

I think about the Poe collection on the bookstore floor. "Remember when we had our picnic at Stevens? Did you tell Blake we talked about that Edgar Allan Poe story?"

Gavin nods. "He asked a lot of questions about our conversations."

"What about the psychology books—the order my mother placed?"

"That was Blake, too," Zoey says. "He said you showed him how to do special orders."

The deceit was like a chess game to him. I feel exhausted, and it makes me remember the medicine in Blake's room with Zoey's name on it. "There was a prescription bottle—"

"I wondered where those pills went," she says. "Sometimes I need them to sleep."

He drugged me—he must have. The more I think about it, the more I'm sure. No wonder he could get into my room and leave handprints without waking me.

I mentally run through the other odd events of the past days, like how Norma said someone complained about noise. Blake probably called her. It had to be him. That would give her an excuse to show up, and he knew that would spook me. How many other ways had he manipulated me?

"He followed me to the cemetery, right?"

Zoey nods. "He texted me a photo of a muddy handprint. I mimicked that on the mirror. Then I left one in the laundry room. He knew you'd never suspect him because he was with you."

"What about the black flowers? Did he leave those?"

She scrunches her mouth, looking puzzled. "No, that doesn't sound familiar."

"Did he ever say anything about moving a photo of my dad?"

She shakes her head.

I'm surprised, but Blake might not have told her all the details. Zoey and Gavin didn't even realize what the other one was up to. Blake likes to control everything, including the information he shares.

"Look," Gavin says. "Maybe we should call the police."

I consider it. "We don't have any concrete proof, though. Is any of this even criminal? He took the bookstore money from the register, but then left it in my purse."

"That one was risky," Zoey says. "He planted it ahead of time, but you didn't notice the envelope until you were at the store."

"Why would he do that?" I'm in shock. "He is *crazy*. Absolutely crazy. The amount of planning he put into conning me—"

"He's a sociopath," Zoey says, as calmly as if she were describing his sense of humor or the way he drives. "It's all a big game to him. Everything is about winning. But he can be incredibly irresistible when he wants."

A big game. I'm just a pawn he maneuvered in some bizarre scenario he set up.

"He didn't really lose his keys," I say.

She digs through her purse and tosses them to me. I tuck them in my backpack, happy that she can't intrude anymore.

Gavin's phone pings. "We've got a problem. I just received a text. It's from you, El."

"Let me see." I read my supposed text to Gavin aloud. "*I can't believe you broke up with me like that. I never want to see you again.* He's got the first part right."

We sit in silence, except for the tapping of Zoey's heels as she paces. She reminds me of a caged leopard at the zoo.

"Let's think this through," I say. "Is he trying to make sure we don't get back together?"

Zoey pauses. "I think you're missing the point. He's got your phone. He's texting people as you."

"Ugh. You're right. He can cause all kinds of trouble. We'll need to get it turned off."

"I'll check how to do that online," Gavin says.

While Gavin works on the phone problem, I try to make more sense of Blake's actions. "Zoey, what about Oscar? Did he really make him bleed everywhere?"

"I don't know who Oscar is, but we searched for fake blood recipes on my phone. You mix water, corn syrup, corn starch, and food coloring."

Fake blood. At least I can be thankful it wasn't the real thing.

Zoey's phone rings. "I don't recognize this number." She holds up the phone for us to see.

"He's calling from my cell." I consider grabbing the phone and screaming at him. But it's better if he doesn't realize everything I've learned.

Gavin gives her a stern look. "You can't tell him El is here."

She plops down on the couch next to me and answers the call. If she says one wrong thing, I plan on ripping the phone out of her manicured hands.

"Hi, baby. Where are you calling from? Oh, bummer. I'm sure it'll turn up. Yeah, lunch sounds great. See you soon."

Zoey hangs up with a grin. "Not that I'm going anywhere," she says, stretching her legs out on the coffee table. "I do like to imagine him waiting there for me."

He won't wait for long before moving to the next part of his plan, whatever that is.

"Here," Gavin says to me. "You need to enter some info for the cell company to turn off your phone."

I take a few minutes to fill out the form and submit it. With this done, Blake can't pretend to be me any longer. Still, I feel uneasy, like we're missing something. I'm about to hand Gavin back his phone, but it rings first: the animal shelter.

"El, it's Skyler. A guy called about a cat named Oscar that was surrendered by mistake. He said it's his cat, that he's coming to get him with proof of ownership."

My stomach twists. I can't believe Blake figured out that Oscar was at the shelter. Then again, I shouldn't be surprised after everything I've learned. What proof of ownership does he have? Vet records?

The exact details don't matter. He would not get another chance to harm my cat. "Don't let anyone take him. I'll be there in five minutes."

I grab my backpack. "I have to reach Oscar before Blake does."

Gavin looks at Zoey.

"What?" she says.

"You have to meet Blake. You can stall him, give El more time."

"Why would I do that?"

"Come on. After all the crap you did? I think you owe her."

She stands and stretches. "Fine. I might as well get the breakup over with."

Gavin grabs his keys. "I'll go with you, El." His voice is gentle, apologetic. "Let me help."

"No, that's not a good idea," I say. "There's something else I need you to take care of."

# 31

# HOME

I can't let anything happen to Oscar. He's the last connection to my life before Blake destroyed it. I don't know what taking Oscar would do for him, but at this point, his twisted logic doesn't matter.

I try to piece together everything Zoey and Gavin told me as I jog to the shelter. The records from the psychiatric hospital were fake—Mom never lied about Dad. There was no reason to. The ghostly handprints were also fake. I don't know how he found Dad's photo. He could have somehow left the black flowers, too, I guess. It seems doubtful that Zoey would know all of his tricks.

As I enter the shelter, I realize I know most of what Blake did, and how, but I'm still struggling with why. The planning, his manipulation, my total cluelessness—it must have been fun for him. I told him I secretly believed in ghosts. How amusing for him to take advantage of that.

He obviously made up the story about me cheating on his friend. That could be a cover for his real motive. Maybe he was jealous about our family dinner, furious over Stanley moving on after Blake and his mom struggled for years—furious enough to leave the restaurant without even letting us know he was there.

I may never completely understand.

Once I arrive at the shelter, Skyler acts like a spy on a covert mission. She lines an opaque carrier with an old towel. Oscar meows but lets me put him inside with some nuggets of food.

"The vet checked him," she says. "Other than his lethargy, Oscar seems all right."

That's one thing to be grateful for.

The whole escape from the shelter only takes a few minutes. I divide my attention between soothing Oscar and checking the streets for Blake. At least Oscar is unharmed and I have an ally in Gavin. I need to talk to Grace, though. No matter what our issues, she'll help when she hears about Mom.

*Mom.* I ache to talk to her. I may have to call all of the hospitals in Paris to track her down, but I can do it.

First, I have to focus on avoiding Blake, on feeling safe again. I swallow the lump in my throat and keep walking. One block from the shelter, Oscar's carrier already feels like lugging a boulder. I have to keep going.

I glance around, think I spot Blake near the pharmacy, but can't tell for sure. I walk faster, because it almost seems too easy. He calls the shelter, but I rescue Oscar in time. Maybe he did it to force me out of wherever I was hiding, so he could continue his plan to have me committed.

Returning home feels too risky. I head for Hoboken Daycare instead. When I reach the entrance, there's still no sign of him. Taking a deep breath, I prepare to deal with Grace.

The daycare staff know me well enough to buzz me in, and I hurry inside, confident that Blake can't follow. Grace looks up from cleaning crayon marks off a table. She's definitely surprised to see me.

"El, your last text—"

"It wasn't me. Blake has my phone. So much has happened . . ." I want to tell her about Mom's accident, but I can't find the words. "It's a long story. Can I go to your house for a while? I need someplace to stay."

"I would say yes, but Mom's hosting a huge church luncheon. She'll have a fit if you show up with Oscar. Why are you carrying him around, anyway?"

"Blake made him sick. Blake did a lot of things, actually, to make me miserable. Maybe if you come with me, you can explain to your mom how important this is?"

"I can't." Grace clasps and unclasps her hands. "I know it was wrong of me to pretend I wasn't with you that morning. He said it was for a psychology research paper—that you'd know the truth in a few days. It was only a temporary prank, but he needed to record your response for some study he was conducting. I felt horrible afterwards. Didn't you get my text?"

"No, and there was no study. Almost everything Blake says is a lie."

"I thought it was real with him, El. I'm such an idiot. I realized too late, after I was such a jerk to you."

Oscar starts to meow. "I need to go."

"I'm so sorry. I'll call you later, I promise."

It's hard to meet her eyes. I remember what Blake told me over lunch yesterday: She doesn't seem like a good friend. That may be the only true thing he's ever said.

Since I can't bring Oscar to Grace's house, I decide to take my chances and go home. Oscar won't want to stay confined much longer. As I trudge along, I play it all over again in my mind. Blake managed to manipulate Grace, Gavin, and me. I could almost see how Gavin would take the money to date me, how that would feel harmless to him. A few dates, easy cash. I do believe that he started to care about me and that Blake took advantage of that, practically blackmailing him into ending our relationship. He wouldn't be happy if Gavin actually liked me and if events were out of his hands. Because if there's one thing I've learned about Blake, it's that he likes to be in control.

I arrive at my building and, so far, no sign of Blake. I have both sets of his keys, but he could easily sweet-talk Norma into letting him in. If he's already home, I'm in trouble. I hold my breath as the elevator doors open, thankful it's empty. Outside our apartment door, I strain to listen.

I hear a guy's voice from inside the apartment. My heart races. I'll have to take my chances at Grace's house or with Henry at the bookstore. Before I can sneak away, Oscar begins meowing loudly. He must recognize that we're home.

"Shh," I whisper. "Please, please be quiet."

Did Blake hear us?

I'm about to rush for the elevator when the door opens. I inhale sharply and nearly drop Oscar.

Mom stands before me, in perfect health.

# 32

# REALITY

Sobbing, I set the cat carrier down, then rush into Mom's arms. I wonder for a moment if I really am having a breakdown.

Mom holds me tight as an equally uninjured Stanley hovers near us.

"Thank goodness you're all right," he says. "We've been frantic with worry. You didn't answer your cell—"

"It's missing because—"

"Or answer the home phone," Stanley interrupts. "We've left multiple messages. When we arrived after the whole confusion with our flight, we found blood all over your room. Blake and his things were gone, and you were missing, too. We were about to call the police."

Mom wipes her eyes as she nods in agreement. "I thought something horrible had happened."

"I can explain. But first, what happened to you? A woman called from Paris and said you were in a horrible accident. Blake spoke to her." Even as I'm saying it, it dawns on me that it was part of Blake's intricate scheme. One phone call and our parents are critically injured. There's no proof other than his conversation in a foreign language. Why would I have wanted proof? He would've counted on my believing him.

Actually, no. I bet he had a backup plan. A made-up hospital report or news article—as fake as Dad's psychiatric records.

Oscar's meowing reaches a frantic pitch. When I let him out, he scampers away, grateful to be free. Beyond weary, I collapse onto the couch. Mom joins me while Stanley stands, wringing his hands.

"He told you we were in the hospital?" Mom says. "We were delayed, but Stanley let him know. Somehow the reservation was moved to a different flight. We thought you knew about the setback, too. I had no idea . . ." She seems at a loss for words.

Their travel plans got messed up. Blake knew it. Another lightbulb moment: He didn't just know it. He *caused* it.

"What would someone need to switch a flight reservation?" I ask.

"I don't know," Mom said. "Probably the credit card number and the original flight information."

Or a girlfriend who works for the airlines.

"Why?" Mom asks.

"It must have been Blake," I say. "He must have changed the flight."

"Why in the world would he do that?" Stanley asks. "You better tell us what's going on."

Sitting safely on the couch next to Mom, I do my best to summarize everything Blake's done over the past week. I'm barely finished when someone buzzes to be let in.

I rush to the speaker before they do. "Who is it?"

"I'm here about the locks," a gruff voice says.

Gavin did as I asked and arranged for the locks to be replaced. He came through for me. "I need to keep Blake out," I explain to Mom and Stanley, buzzing in the locksmith.

Stanley nods, but his face is pale, like he's in shock. He wanders into their bedroom and closes the door.

When the locksmith finishes, Mom pays him and makes arrangements for the bookstore locks to be changed, too. We order Chinese food for dinner, and Stanley joins us at the table. He doesn't say much, but he shovels the food into his mouth like he's pissed.

Stanley's anger doesn't matter, because it's so good to just look at Mom, to realize that she's fine. It feels like we should talk about their honeymoon, but the situation with Blake has taken its toll. His manipulations are all I can think about.

"Norma must have let Blake back into the apartment to get his stuff," I say, "because I had his keys."

"I'll let Norma know what's going on," Mom says. "Maybe we should have her change the building lock, just in case."

"I checked with Veronique." Stanley's voice is seething.

"She hasn't heard from Blake. I wonder where he is now. At NYU? You've locked him out, destroyed his phone."

Mom bristles. "Have you been listening to Ella? He faked papers about her father to make her think he died in a mental hospital. He broke into the bookstore and left handprints on walls so she would think she was going crazy. Why would he do such a thing? We might need a restraining order, Stanley."

"That's ludicrous!"

"Not to Ella. And not to me, either."

The rest of dinner is incredibly tense as they continue their heated discussion. I eat my veggies and rice as fast as possible. Grace calls, as promised, but I can't possibly talk on the kitchen phone in the middle of Mom and Stanley's argument. We hang up quickly. Then I grab cleaning supplies and head for my room.

I sit on my bare mattress and survey the mess. The fact that the blood is fake makes the job easier. Oscar watches me from the bookcase, a comforting presence.

Mom joins me with clean sheets to make my bed. "It's fake blood," I explain. "It comes right off."

"That's one good thing," Mom says. "I took pictures, you know. For when we report this to the police."

"Stanley doesn't seem convinced we should do anything about this." I can't control the bitterness in my voice.

"He'll come around. I think he's in shock that his son could be so cruel. We'll decide on our next steps tomorrow, after a good night's rest. I'm sorry about everything that you've been through. I had no idea." She pauses. "Well, that's not completely true. I thought something was odd when he cut himself on the broken plate that night. I could swear he did it on purpose. I thought I must've been overreacting, though. I mean, who would do such a thing? It was senseless. We were so happy that Blake was making an effort after all these years of being angry at Stanley. But this . . . this is unbelievable." She unfolds the fitted sheet. "Grab an end."

I take the bottom while she pulls the top around the mattress.

"Where is Stanley?" I ask.

"Sorting through the mail, paying bills. It's not his fault, you know. I think he's as horrified as we are."

I doubt that.

We lay the flat sheet on the bed. I smooth out the wrinkles while Mom tucks in the edges. "What's this?" Her hand is between the box spring and the mattress.

"What?"

Mom pulls out a large sealed baggie. It's filled with cash.

# 33

# THE PRESENT

Monday morning, I wake to the sound of Mom and Stanley arguing about the cash under my mattress. I stand behind my closed door to listen, inches from my assortment of cat pictures. Staring at the happy cats, the sad cats, it strikes me that the whole collage is immature. Prying up the corner of a photo, I pull. It makes a satisfying ripping sound.

"Someone wrote out checks to 'cash' and forged my signature. Now Ella has the money. What other proof do you need?" Stanley yells in the other room.

Mom's voice is lower but full of fury. "It's convenient that he tried to have her declared mentally incompetent before he disappeared. Maybe he hid some of the money there to make her look guilty. Where's the rest of it? And where is Blake?"

*Good question.* I channel my nervous energy into digging my nail under some of the mischievous cats and peeling them off.

"Why don't you ask your daughter?" Stanley asks.

"Sure, right after I call the police about your son."

"Well, that's going to take a lot of convincing. It's a bit of he-said-she-said, isn't it? And she has at least part of the money," Stanley says. "Ella confessed to finding the bookstore cash in her own bag. She's framing him, not the other way around."

The back of my door is now blank. I save my three favorite cat pictures and dump the rest in the trash. No wonder Blake wanted me to go to a psychiatric hospital. No one would ever believe me if I were declared insane.

Now, with the money he planted, Mom won't call the police if it means I'll be implicated in any kind of theft, even though Stanley got some of the money back. She won't take the chance.

Stanley takes the day off from work. I expect him to yell at me during breakfast, but he's oddly quiet after the argument with Mom, then leaves on an errand without saying good-bye. Once she and I are finally alone in the kitchen, I ask her what's going on.

"Stanley called NYU."

"Blake's there?" I ask, eager for him to be found. Not knowing where he's staying gives me the chills. I'll feel better once we know exactly where he disappeared to.

"No, he's not at the university," she says. "As a matter of fact, they've never heard of him. His tuition payment was never cashed."

I shouldn't be surprised to learn that Blake was never accepted at NYU—that he's not a registered student. I know what he's capable of, and yet I'm still shocked.

If he's not at college, where is he? Blake knew Mom and Stanley would finally arrive home and that at least some of his lies would be exposed. I'm sure he made an exit plan, but I can't figure out what it might be. It leaves me unsettled.

Later that day, Mom finds me in my room. "We should buy you a new phone. I don't like the idea that you can't reach me if you're out." She notices the back of the door. "Oh! Your collage is gone."

"I need to change my room. I'd like to paint it, too, maybe a more golden shade of yellow."

"Ella, now isn't the time for a project like this."

"Now is exactly the time," I say. "Blake was in my room, this version of it, while I was sleeping. He put fake blood on my walls. It makes perfect sense to repaint them."

"It's a big job. You need the paint, the drop cloths—"

"I know, Mom."

"I don't think picking out paint is on our list for today."

"It's on *my* list." I want to choose it myself. As much as I hate arguing with Mom, I won't back down this time. "I have a friend at the hardware store. He'll help me. You won't have to do anything."

She puts up her hands in surrender. "All right. Can you be ready to leave in fifteen minutes?"

"Sounds perfect."

After I pick a new phone, we walk to the library, where I check out two nonfiction books that I slip into my bag before Mom can notice. While I wait for her, I text Gavin to thank him for taking care of the locks and tell him about Oscar's safe recovery and Mom returning home. I mention stopping by to pick out paint, and he says he'd like to see me. As much as I'm worried about Blake, I convince Mom to let me go to the hardware store alone.

"You need to be careful, Ella, until we figure out where Blake is. We don't know what he is capable of. Text me frequently so I know you're fine. You can't over-communicate in a situation like this."

I reluctantly agree.

When I enter the store, Gavin's making keys. I can't help clenching my fists for a moment at the memory of him copying all of mine for Blake.

"I'll be done in a few minutes," he says when he notices me. "The paint swatches are in the first aisle if you want to start looking."

There are more shades of yellow than I ever imagined. I've narrowed it down to Daffodil, Candlelight, or Haystack when Gavin joins me. I hug him hello but back away before he can kiss me.

"Thanks again for arranging the locks," I say.

"It's the least I could do. Have you heard anything from Blake?"

"No. We can't figure out where he is. Did Zoey meet him for lunch?"

Gavin shakes his head. "He blew her off at the last minute,

said he was meeting a friend, some guy named Martin. Zoey's convinced it's really another girl."

I remember Blake's list of phone contacts. There was no Martin. There were no friends at all, actually.

"I'll feel better when we know where he is."

"Me, too."

I show him the three paint colors. "Which do you like best?"

He points. "Haystack."

The name reminds me of the odds of finding Blake, but it's my favorite, too.

Gavin figures out how many gallons I'll need. He offers to use his employee discount and bring the paint and supplies over tomorrow. Another customer comes over to ask about wing nuts, which saves us from an awkward good-bye.

After texting Mom as proof of life, I stop at the bakery for a box of cat-shaped cookies, then head to the shelter to thank Skyler for her help. I detour to the cattery to visit Petals first.

She's nowhere to be found. Not in the cages, or the beds, or the carpeted cubbies that I frantically check.

My stomach drops as I remember Stanley mentioning Petals at dinner that first night Blake was home. *No.* Blake wouldn't have taken her, would he?

"Skyler!" I run through the shelter, bouncing the stupid cookies. "Skyler!" I finally find her in the kennels among the barking dogs.

"What's the matter?" she asks. "Has something else happened to Oscar?"

"He's fine." My voice cracks. "Petals?"

"It's great news—an old man adopted her."

"Really?" Relief floods through me. "Thank goodness."

"He said he's changing her name to Petunia, though, after the flower."

"Except she's pure black."

"That's what I thought!" Skyler says. "Weird, right?"

I'm happy she finally found a home, but I wish I'd gotten a chance to see her one last time. "Any other adoptions?"

"Two of the kittens from Jersey City, Goedal and Mink, found homes fast. Oh, and a little boy came in with his mom and fell in love with Milo. He was about six years old and never had a pet before. It was the cutest thing ever."

I smile, imagining their joy. We catch up a bit on other shelter business until I can't stand the barking anymore and say good-bye. I text Mom to let her know I'm fine. The scare of thinking Blake took Petals keeps me hyper-focused as I hurry. A woman passes me, walking four well-behaved dogs. A man Stanley's size jogs by with his headphones so loud I can hear the dance music. There are lots of people, but no sign of Blake.

Back at home, I prepare my room for painting. I carefully place a line of masking tape along the ceiling and move everything away from the walls. Mom pokes her head in.

"You're really going through with this?"

"I know Dad painted it originally, but it's time for a

change. Gavin said he'd help me." I've told her enough about Gavin that she's letting him visit tomorrow.

"All right," she says.

I can tell she's not entirely convinced, but it's my room. My decision.

Once she's gone, I take the library books out of my messenger bag and spend most of the evening reading about sociopaths. According to the experts, sociopaths often leave a trail of destruction behind them. I'm basically fine, though I'm not so sure about Stanley and Mom. No abyss has formed, not yet, but there are definite fissures in their relationship. Overall, I'm lucky I made it through my time with Blake relatively unscathed.

The next day, I decide to go to the cemetery before Mom can give me another safety lecture. After washing up, I reach into my drawer of cat shirts for a clean one. My fingers brush against plastic.

It's another bag of cash that Blake must have planted.

I'm not telling Stanley—it'll make him doubt me even more. Maybe I'll tell Mom. Maybe not. I tuck the bag under the FREEDOM ROCKS shirt, then close the drawer.

After dressing in a pretty blouse instead, I leave Mom a note so she won't worry and head to the cemetery. It's a relief to visit Dad knowing that Mom had been truthful all along. I search the ground for the right pebble and place it on his tombstone. The muddy handprint has faded, of course. Still, the thought of Blake following me makes me uneasy, like someone is watching right now.

I glance around frantically to check for Blake. Instead of my stepbrother, Henry approaches. He's holding a fistful of familiar black flowers.

"Good morning, Ella."

"Hi. I've noticed those flowers here before. They're unusual."

Henry smiles. "Black cat petunias. I thought Thomas would like the name. I grow them myself."

I nod. "Why are you visiting Dad? I mean, I know you're related, but . . ."

"It's the guilt, I guess, that brings me here."

"The guilt?"

"I arranged that meeting the night he died," he says. "Didn't your mother ever tell you?"

I shake my head.

"I was on a mission to recruit him that day. It was a good position, working with me at the American Veterinary Medical Association. He could've really made a difference in deciding the training of future vets." He sighs. "Thomas told me no immediately. Working with families and their pets, that's what he said he was meant to do, what he imagined his life to be."

"Mom always said that he loved his job."

"True, but I didn't take his rejection very well. I told him he was capable of more, that he was . . . well, I accused him of being stubborn. We didn't leave on good terms. I had convinced him to at least meet the association president that evening, to learn more about the opportunity."

He leans one hand on the tombstone, as if summoning his strength. "He agreed to the meeting, but still turned the job down. That's where he was leaving from, the night of the accident. It was my fault."

I pat Henry's shoulder in an attempt to comfort him. "It's not like you were driving the car that killed my father."

"True. But I might as well have been. The regret . . ." He sighs. "I've always wished I could take back our last conversation. Being around you—I can barely look at you without thinking of him. I'm sorry if I've been unkind, Ella. Memories can be painful. I realized after the break-in that if something bad happened to you, too, I'd have more to be ashamed of."

"It's okay," I say. And it is. It's good to finally discover why Henry has been grumpy toward me. "I'm sure Dad understood, you know."

"Maybe." He gently places the black flowers on the grave. "I can't stay long. I have a new cat to get home to."

I stare at the petunias. And it hits me. "You're the one who adopted Petals."

"Black Cat Petunia," he says. "She's a sweet girl."

"I love that cat. She was my favorite."

"You can visit her sometime, if you want."

"Really? That would be amazing!" I smile at the thought of seeing Petals again.

When Henry turns to go, I decide not to linger in the cemetery alone. I press my hand against Dad's grave before Henry and I leave together.

When Gavin arrives to help me with my room, Mom stares at his blue hair but doesn't say anything about it. He comes prepared with the paint supplies and lunch from Veggie Paradise.

"I'll be in my room if you need me," Mom says. "I'll take Oscar so we don't end up with golden paw prints everywhere."

Gavin and I work out a system where he paints the edges of the walls with a brush, and I roll the main parts. The color looks amazing—cheerful and bright, exactly what I wanted.

"I hope you like the falafel sandwiches I brought," Gavin says. "I'm trying a vegetarian diet for a month. It's the least I can do after lying to you." He paints around the outside of my closet. "How are you doing?"

"I'm fine. And Oscar made a full recovery. He'll be happier once we're finished, and he can return to his favorite spot on top of the bookshelf."

When I put the roller down to refill the tray, Gavin takes my hands in his, both of us speckled with Haystack. "El, I know I said this before. I'm sorry I was part of his lies. I should've found a way to be honest with you."

"It's all right."

"I brought you a present," he says.

"Really?"

He pulls something from his pocket—a flash of black. "It's just a little something. I found it in the store below my cousin's apartment." He opens his palm to show me the obsidian ring, the one with the carved flower I had been admiring when Grace and I went to have our Tarot card readings. HELPS CONTACT WITH THE SPIRIT WORLD, the label still reads.

I shiver. What are the odds he would pick the black flower ring?

"You forgive me?" His eyes are soft, pleading.

The ring is a good sign. And I like him, I really do. But forgiveness will take time.

I make eye contact, keep my face neutral and my voice even, just like I learned from Blake. "Of course I forgive you."

The lie comes easily. Maybe Blake has damaged me after all.

After I put my room back together, I flip through one of the library books again. There's a section I want to reread about a sociopath's desire to win. I leaf through the pages slowly, scanning the text. At page eighty-eight I find it.

Not the section. A photo stuck between the pages.

The photo of Dad has reappeared.

Blake couldn't have put it there. There's no way he had access to the hiding spot in my closet in the last twenty-four hours or to my library book. He might be devious, but this was beyond his capabilities. Gavin was in my room, but never alone, and he didn't know anything about the photo.

No, this is from Dad. Just like it was his voice that called out to me and saved me from being hit by that car years ago. The certainty settles over me. I sit quietly, holding the picture, letting its reappearance sink in.

I think back to the other page eighty-eight in the cat memoir. It had been about violence toward cats. I shudder, remembering fake blood–covered Oscar, wondering what Blake would have done with him after I left. It couldn't have been a coincidence that the photo was on that page.

I put it on my nightstand for now, then turn back to the library book. Page eighty-eight is about sociopaths and their dangerous charm. Blake is certainly charming. I think about the dress he bought for me, how he wanted Mom's wedding present to be just right. But he didn't care about us—it was all a pretense. Everything he did was phony, even details like the NYU catalog on his nightstand.

There had been a travel guide with the course catalog, too, something about Spanish-speaking travel destinations. It had to be another attempt to mislead me. Blake spoke French, and I doubt he would flee to someplace where he couldn't lie fluently.

What else do I know about him that might be true? I remember the night we sat on the bench: He loves the ocean and chess. *Deux vérités*. Would he go to the south of France? Maybe. Or an exotic island somewhere? On a whim, I do a search on my new phone: Caribbean Islands. French speaking. There are a few matches, including St. Martin and Martinique.

*Martin.* Blake had told Zoey he would visit a friend named Martin. He thought he was so clever. He couldn't have known that the throwaway line would get back to me. I expand my search to include one more Blake-related item: chess.

Martinique is the only result that highlights all three. I read an article about the island, how it has its own chess federation and even hosted a major tournament a few years back. Martinique looks like a beautiful place to escape to.

He couldn't have disappeared without a trace. If Mom and Stanley decide not to involve the police, maybe I'll hire a private investigator on my own to find Blake. The irony of using the money he planted to track him down appeals to me.

I plug the phone into the charger next to my bed. Dad's photo hasn't moved from where I left it. I pick it up, ready to stash the picture again. I pause, considering.

Instead of hiding it away, I dig through the hall closet near Mom's room, the one where she stores a random assortment of candles, the bread machine she never uses, and a collection of frames. I find one the right size, silver with a raised paw print in the corner. I place the picture inside and gaze at the result.

Dad is smiling away from the camera as if he knows a wonderful secret. When Mom captured that moment, I believe he was daydreaming about me, the daughter he would always love.

# ACKNOWLEDGMENTS

Like the fictional Oscar, this novel had about nine lives. I transformed version after version, making major changes along the way, but one of the few details that stayed the same was that Ella's mom owns a bookstore. A very special thanks to Jonah and [words] Bookstore in Maplewood, New Jersey, for allowing me to visit behind the scenes during a busy holiday season, and to Carrie for the crash course in their bookstore operations. (Any errors in portraying an indie bookstore are obviously my own.)

Thanks to Dr. Philip Ernest Schoenberg from Ghosts of NY, and Professor of History at Vaughn College. I had the pleasure of going on the Ghosts of NY Indoor Ghost Walk of Grand Central Station. Dr. Schoenberg kindly gave me permission to adapt a ghost story from that tour for my fictional train station haunting in Chapter 18.

Thank you to Julie Matysik for acquiring *Black Flowers, White Lies* and for sharing her thoughtful editorial vision, and to Sky Pony Press's Rachel Stark for continuing the process. Thanks to Sarah Brody, Joshua Barnaby, Cheryl Lew, and the rest of the Sky Pony team for transforming my manuscript into a beautiful book. Having my second novel published by the Sky Pony/Skyhorse team and distributed by the Perseus sales force felt like coming home.

I am fortunate to be represented by Liza Fleissig of the Liza Royce Agency. Liza is a positive, energetic, responsive force in a business filled with ups and downs. It was meant to be, Liza!

Publicizing a book is a very different process from writing one. Rebecca Grose (and Sammie) of SoCal Public Relations—we get to do it again! I'm thankful for my fellow writers in Kidlit Authors Club, UncommonYA, NJAN, and to the private online groups who have provided a sense of comradery. Thanks to Jennifer Halligan of JHPR for helping to get the word out about my novels.

The Whiteley family (Michael, Claudia, Danny) runs the amazing Isshinryu Karate dojo in Madison and Bernardsville, New Jersey. Special thanks to my sensei, Claudia Whiteley, for reminding me to keep my head up (literally and figuratively) and for continuing to be an inspiration to me. To Ann, Anne, Ariadne, Aviva, and Emi: thanks for the dog walks and the friendship. I'm grateful to all my dojo friends and training partners for their support.

I'm thankful for the creative understanding and encouragement of my writer friends, particularly Maria Andreu, Charlotte Bennardo, Susan Brody, Lisa Colozza Cocca, and Natalie Zaman, who also provided advice on several of my otherworldly scenes. Thank you to Steve Meltzer for the brainstorming and to the many NJ SCBWI members I reunite with each year at the annual conference. Thanks to Katherine Clark and Anthony Oakes for research help during early drafts. Too many people to list read prior versions of this story and provided insightful feedback—know that I am grateful to you all.

Thanks to my cat-loving friends for sharing their photos, especially author Jennifer Murgia and her real-life Oscar. Thank you to the Rolling Hill Book Club for their interest in the writing life and for their love of good books. Thanks to the Pfizer Madison Toastmasters Club for critiquing my many book-related speeches.

Much gratitude to my incredible critique partners: Melissa Higgins, C. Lee McKenzie, and Heather Strum. LK Madigan read earlier versions of this story. I like to think she'd be pleased I stuck with it.

Much love to my family, always: Shirley, Peter, Amanda, William, Liza, Ken, Rachele, Julio, Julianna, Ryan, JC, Doreen, John, and Skyler Schwartz, our honorary family member. To Chris, Lauren, and David: you bring the joy that makes everything else possible.

# BEHIND THE SCENES OF BLACK FLOWERS, WHITE LIES

Here are some behind-the-scenes facts about the creation of *Black Flowers, White Lies:*

- The original title for *Black Flowers, White Lies* was *In the Dark*, but when Yvonne and her editor realized there were several other books by that title, they decided to change it. The new title inspired the cover design.
- The Feline Historical Museum that Ella mentions in Chapter 2 really exists in Alliance, Ohio. For more information, visit their website: www.felinehistoricalfoundation.org/museum.html.
- Like Ella, Yvonne once had her Tarot cards read by a blind man. He predicted that she would write about sports, which hasn't come true . . . yet. The cards mentioned in Ella's reading are loosely based on the Strength and the Moon cards.
- During the writing of *Black Flowers, White Lies*, Yvonne asked her cat-owning friends for their pets' names and incorporated many of them into the story, including her editor's mischievous cat, Azula. Except for Petals, all of the shelter cats are named after real animals.

- The novel references several Hoboken ghost stories about Arthur's Tavern, The Brass Rail, and Stevens Institute of Technology. The haunting set in the PATH station that Gavin describes to Ella is actually based on a story about NYC's Grand Central Station.

- Even though the title isn't specifically mentioned in *Black Flowers, White Lies,* the book on Ella's nightstand about the grumpy man who adopts a cat was inspired by the memoir *The Cat Who Came for Christmas* by Cleveland Amory.

- In Chapter 27, Ella meets Gavin at Sybil's Cave. A real-life murder of Mary Rogers near that location in 1841 inspired Edgar Allan Poe's story, "The Mystery of Marie Rogêt."

- Black cat petunias (like those that appear by the tombstone in the novel) are hard to find in gardening stores, but Yvonne ordered several plants online and grew them in her garden. The petals start out as a deep purple and darken over time.

- When Yvonne first tried the recipe in Chapter 30, she used corn oil instead of corn syrup (not the same thing!). The result was messy until she figured out the wrong ingredient.

- A former Hoboken resident, Yvonne visited the New Jersey city several times during the writing of *Black Flowers, White Lies* for further research. She has a Pinterest board of setting-related photos at www.pinterest.com/yvonneventresca/hoboken-new-jersey.

# BLACK FLOWERS, WHITE LIES: AN EDUCATOR'S GUIDE

Below are some sample discussion questions for educators. The complete guide aligns with many ELA Common Core standards, including: Writing, Language, Speaking and Listening (grades 7–12), Reading for Information (grades 7–8), and Reading Literature (grades 9–12). Special thanks to Marcie Colleen for creating this guide to help educators use *Black Flowers, White Lies* for classroom study, book clubs, and independent reading.

To download a free copy of the complete educator's guide, containing over fifty discussion points, activities, and writing prompts, visit Yvonne's website at YvonneVentresca.com.

- Authors often begin novels at a point of conflict or change in the life of the protagonist. What is changing in Ella's life that would be considered a point of conflict at the beginning of the book?

- Ella says, "being in the cemetery brings me peace, quiets the anxious thoughts that often scurry through my mind." Explain what she might mean by this. Why might Ella's recent visit to the cemetery disappoint her mother?

- Shortly after Blake arrives, he says he always wanted a sister. At that point in the story, how is Blake being a good brother to Ella? After you've reached the end of the novel, how do you view that same behavior?
- Ella chooses to wear the rose-colored dress her mother picked out for her instead of the strapless, yellow dress Blake bought for her. Do you think she made the right choice? Why or why not?
- When Gavin visits the shelter, Ella thinks he is not being entirely honest. What are some of the red flags that raise her suspicions? Did you think he might be lying when you read this chapter? Why or why not?
- Do you believe Ella's accounts of what has happened? If not, she might be an "unreliable narrator." What books or movies have unreliable narrators? How does the reliability of the narrator affect the reader's or the viewer's experience?
- Many of the characters in *Black Flowers, White Lies* try to deceive each other. Blake lies about his early arrival into town. Ella hides the truth when Grace asks her about Blake and Beautiful Boy. And Ella's mother kept a big secret for much of Ella's life regarding Oscar. Select one character and trace their lies throughout the story. Did learning about their dishonesty surprise you? If not, what clues are there in the text that they might not be telling the truth? At what point did you find yourself catching on to the fact that they might be lying?

- If you were Ella, what evidence and other items would you want to take with you when you escaped the apartment? Explain why you chose each item.
- Throughout the story, Ella believes that Henry doesn't like her. What does she learn about Henry in the final chapter? Have you ever learned additional facts about a person that made you reevaluate your initial opinion of them?
- How has Ella changed from the beginning of the novel to the end?

# FURTHER READING

*In Sheep's Clothing: Understanding and Dealing with Manipulative People* by George K. Simon, Jr., PhD

*The Sociopath Next Door* by Martha Stout, PhD

"Sybil's Cave History." Hoboken Historical Museum, www.hobokenmuseum.org/self-guided-walking-tours/ sybils-cave-history

*Without Conscience: The Disturbing World of the Psychopaths Among Us* by Robert D. Hare, PhD

# ABOUT THE AUTHOR

© Countryside Studios

In addition to *Black Flowers, White Lies*, Yvonne Ventresca is the author of the young adult novel *Pandemic*, winner of a Crystal Kite Award from the Society of Children's Book Writers and Illustrators.

Yvonne has also written two non-fiction books, *Avril Lavigne* (a biography of the singer) and *Publishing* (about careers in the field). Several of her short stories have been selected for anthologies: "Justice for Jaynie" in *30 Shades of Dead*, "The Art of Remaining Bitter" in *Hero Lost: Mysteries of Death and Life*, and "Escape to Orange Blossom" in *Prep for Doom*.

Currently a third degree black belt, Yvonne studies Isshinryu karate in a haunted dojo. When she's not creating stories about contagious illnesses, ghosts, or other creepy things, she teaches writing workshops and blogs about the creative life. Her website includes resources for teen writers, comprehensive educator guides for her novels, and upcoming events where you can meet her in person. For more information, visit YvonneVentresca.com.